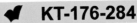

KT-176-284

Staffordshire Library and Inf

Please return or renew or by th

CODSALL

If
in

3 8014 05068 3694

The Sons of Casey O'Donnell

When the outlaw Casey O'Donnell steals $10,000 from the railroad, the townsfolk of Prospect Creek turn against his honest sons, Ryan and Alexander. It takes an act of bravery by Ryan to prove they are their father's sons in name only. But even after Ryan is appointed deputy sheriff, they aren't allowed to enjoy their restored status for long.

Casey returns claiming that even if most of the stories about his outlaw activities are true, he didn't steal the money. Ryan sets out to uncover the truth, but with the discredited railroad man Hudson Gilmore and a gun-toting US marshal on Casey's trail, the mission tests his loyalty to his family to the limit.

The Sons of Casey O'Donnell

Scott Connor

A Black Horse Western

ROBERT HALE · LONDON

ISBN 978-0-7090-9265-0

Robert Hale Limited
Clerkenwell House
Clerkenwell Green
London EC1R 0HT

www.halebooks.com

Typeset by
Derek Doyle & Associates, Shaw Heath
Printed and bound in Great Britain by
CPI Antony Rowe, Chippenham and Eastbourne

CHAPTER 1

'Everyone stay out of this and there'll be no trouble!'

With a stampede of pattering feet the saloon customers backed away from the bar, leaving the two gunslingers standing with guns brandished on either side of the railroad man, Edmond Shaffer.

Ten feet from the bar Ryan O'Donnell was drinking alone at a table. He kept his head down over his whiskey, but from under a lowered brim he ensured he had a good view of the developing situation.

'What do you men want?' Edmond demanded, using a firm voice that showed no hint of fear.

'Time's up,' the nearest gunslinger said. 'You got the warning. Now you're coming with us.'

Edmond narrowed his eyes, his hand straying to his pocket, but the motion made the second man grab his arm then swing him round to face the door. Despite his situation Edmond stood tall and cast his measured gaze across the nearest customers.

'Don't worry about me,' he announced, 'I'll be fine.'

His tone was so confident it made the gunslingers dart worried glances around the saloon room. Their gazes came to rest on the man who was standing two feet beyond the swinging batwings: Sheriff Jerry Harris.

'You will be,' Harris said, 'because you're not leaving with these men.'

The gunslingers considered the sheriff's drawn six-shooter with arrogant sneers.

'There's two of us and one of you, lawman.'

In response Harris settled his stance and so, with the situation about to come to a head, Ryan reckoned this was the right moment for him to make a move. He downed his whiskey, then steadily scraped back his chair, drawing the nearest gunslinger's attention. Then he stood and made his slow way to the bar.

'Stay back,' the gunslinger said.

Ryan walked on for another pace, then came to a sudden halt and flinched as if he'd noticed the situation for the first time.

'I want another drink,' he said with a shrug. 'Be obliged if you'd move aside.'

Ryan's behaviour made several customers snort laughs, but they were silenced when other customers muttered their disapproval.

'Wait there,' the gunslinger said. 'We're not going

anywhere until the sheriff drops his gun.'

Ryan cast Harris a brief glance. 'Don't care about no sheriff. Don't care about no railroad man. Don't care about you. Do care about getting to the bar.'

The gunslinger narrowed his eyes, but Sheriff Harris spoke up first.

'This isn't the time for your antics, Ryan,' he said. 'Sit down.'

Ryan ignored him and moved to reach the bar by slipping between the men, but this provoked the expected reaction. One gunslinger thrust his gun up against Edmond's neck while the other turned his gun on Ryan, making him stop.

'Do you know who I am?' Ryan asked, considering the gun with bored indifference.

The gunslinger firmed his gun hand. 'You're just some unarmed man wasting away his life in a two-bit saloon.'

Ryan shook his head. 'Wrong. I'm Ryan O'Donnell, the eldest son of Casey O'Donnell. You may have heard of him.'

The man's right eye twitched and he cast a glance at his colleague before he got over his surprise with a shake of the head.

'Sure. They say he hightailed it out of the state last year with ten thousand dollars of the railroad's money.'

'He did, and so, as you can probably guess, I'm not a popular man around these parts. That means I don't care none for Prospect Creek and I care even less for railroad men. So get out of my way and let me get to the bar.'

The gunslingers glared at him, but then with a sudden change of heart they both snorted laughs and made mocking gestures, beckoning him on.

Ryan wasted no time in slipping between them and filling his glass to the brim. But before he could turn back someone shouted outside, rapid footfalls sounded, then a gunshot pealed out by the door.

Everyone swung round to see Sheriff Harris stagger forward for a pace, then keel over to reveal a bloodied back. As his shooter briefly moved into view on the boardwalk the sudden change of circumstance made the man with a gun on Edmond shove him on towards the door.

This wasn't the kind of distraction that Ryan would have chosen, but it was the best he'd get, so he wasted no time in hurling the full glass of whiskey into the nearest gunman's face, along with the glass.

The man jerked away batting at his eyes and sending the glass skittering across the bar. Before it had fallen over the other side Ryan lunged for the man's gun hand and wrested the weapon from his grip.

He twisted at the hip as the second gunslinger released Edmond and swung round towards him, but the man moved slowly, as if he were in two minds as to whether to keep his gun on Edmond or confront

Ryan. Before he could make his decision Ryan had planted a slug in his stomach that made him double over. A second more carefully aimed shot to the heart made him drop.

He twisted back and slammed a high shot into the other man's chest that made him forget the whiskey that was stinging his eyes. The man grabbed the bar and clung on for a moment before he slid down to the floor.

The customers dispersed and several men headed to the downed lawman, while outside his shooter beat a hasty retreat. Ryan reckoned he could let others deal with him. He tipped his hat to Edmond, now standing alone and unharmed, then claimed another glass and filled it.

'Obliged,' Edmond said with a relieved sigh. He considered him with his eyebrows raised in surprise. 'And I never thought I'd say that to a son of Casey O'Donnell.'

'As I and my brother keep on saying to anyone who'll listen,' Ryan said raising the glass to his lips, 'we may be the sons of Casey O'Donnell, but we're not him.'

CHAPTER 2

One deputy marshal went down in the first volley of lead.

When the second volley tore out the other two deputies Montgomery Pierce and Daniel McSween, split up and ran to opposite sides of the road while Marshal Granville Coe ran towards the hollow shell of the saloon.

Montgomery pounded on for ten paces before the shooters got him in their sights. Slugs kicked at his heels. Fearing he'd be shot in the back he dived to the ground, then rolled to fetch up behind the inadequate cover of a pile of sacks outside the abandoned mercantile.

Whatever had been in the sacks had rotted, giving them the consistency of loose dirt, and sure enough the bullets that tore into them came slicing out the other side. Montgomery's jacket sleeve kicked as one shot almost holed him, but then to his relief the gunfire petered out.

He risked raising himself to appraise the situation.

A man who had identified himself as Hudson Gilmore along with five other men had launched their effective assault from the derelict stables, which stood at the end of the main drag in the abandoned town of Kendall Springs.

In the centre of the road Mannen Foote lay holed and still. Montgomery had known him for three years and he had been a good friend along with being a decent man. He'd only agreed to become US Marshal Granville Coe's special deputy because he needed the money, but then again so had Montgomery and Daniel.

The marshal had hired them to find the railroad man Edmond Shaffer, who had failed to return to the railroad office in Sumner Point after his trip to Prospect Creek. The clues had led them here, but he hadn't expected that they would ride into an ambush.

The marshal had found refuge within the burnt-out wreck of the saloon, while his third deputy, Daniel, was lying flat on the ground behind a heap of old wagon wheels. They'd rotted down to become a pile of crumbling timber and Montgomery reckoned Daniel's cover was even worse than his own.

He caught Daniel's eye with a wave, pointed to him, then to the saloon, signifying that he'd cover him if he wanted to run there. The ever-optimistic

11

Daniel shook his head and gestured downwards, showing that he'd stay where he was.

Daniel thought for a moment, then made the same gestures as Montgomery had given, encouraging Montgomery to be the one who sought somewhere else to hide. Montgomery started to shake his head, but then a slug pinged into the sack to his side and this time it hadn't been fired from the stables.

He turned as two men jerked backwards into hiding in a ruined building on his side of the road. Worse, the building afforded them adequate protection and beside the structure there were other buildings where they could hole up and from where they could easily pick him off.

Montgomery looked around, sizing up where he could find better cover, but a second slug sliced into the sack only inches from his left hand making that consideration less important than that he just move from here. He leapt to his feet and then hurtled across the road, hoping speed alone would save him.

He'd covered five hurried paces before the shooters got their wits about them and fired. Other men from the stables joined in and lead kicked dust to his side and ahead. In a reflex gesture he ducked down and that made him stumble.

He wheeled his arms, fighting for balance, but he failed to keep upright and ten feet from the wheels he fell full length. Luckily he'd gathered plenty of momentum and when he hit the ground he was able to turn the fall into a roll. He turned over twice until he came to rest beside Daniel in a shower of dust.

'I told you it'd be safer over here,' Daniel said with a grin as lead sliced by overhead.

Montgomery slapped him on the back, then shuffled along to lie beside him in a position where he hoped he'd be hidden from the two groups of gunmen. But from the corner of his eye he saw two men hurry into the derelict shell of the building behind the sacks.

If he'd remained where he was the men would have been able to shoot him in the back. As it was they still ducked down into good covered positions behind a short wall, from where they'd be able to take shots at them.

Daniel had already noted these men and so he and Montgomery took turns to blast at the wall, stopping them from returning fire, for now.

'We have to join the marshal,' Montgomery said when he paused to reload. 'We won't be able to keep them at bay for long.'

Daniel grunted that he agreed, and so after he had reloaded they counted down from three. Then they both splayed quick shots at the men before jumping to their feet and hurrying on to the saloon.

Granville saw them coming and laid down covering fire at the stables while Montgomery and Daniel fired wild shots on the run across the road.

Daniel was three paces ahead of Montgomery and he was moving to leap over a broken barrel when he cried out. He staggered sideways for two paces before his legs buckled and he went to his knees, then on to his front.

Copious blood sluiced from his neck and with a sickening feeling in the guts Montgomery reckoned he could probably do nothing for his friend, but he still slid to a halt beside him and grabbed his arm.

He moved to drag him to his feet, but Daniel was a dead weight. When Montgomery put a hand beneath his chin to raise his head Daniel's blank eyes gave him the impression he had been dead before he'd hit the ground.

Montgomery lowered him to the ground, then set off for the saloon.

From behind the short wall Granville was beckoning him on while darting his gaze from the stables to across the road as he looked out for shooters. He fired at the stables, forcing a man who'd emerged through the door to leap back. For a joyous moment Montgomery reckoned he'd reach the relative safety of the saloon.

He thrust out a hand as he prepared to vault over the wall, but then a hammer blow punched him in the ribs.

A moment later his senses told him he'd been shot, then the saloon seemed to recede from him. He had been only two paces from safety, but now it

14

felt like two miles as he dropped to lie on his unwounded side.

He lay there, trying to gather his strength, but his shallow breaths made him feel as if he were dragging fire into his lungs and his legs had gone numb, probably from the shock. The only movement he could manage was to shove his arms forward. So he dug his fingertips into the dirt and drew himself on.

He advanced for only a foot, and so he had no option other than to move himself on again and then again.

Shouted orders were being delivered and sporadic bursts of gunfire sounded, but they seemed to come from a great distance away. At least the sense of detachment from the gunfight kept the fear at bay and he concentrated on the only thing he could do: moving himself on.

After another five movements the pain in his side spread to his arms, but he was reluctant to inspect the damage. He took steady, shallow breaths before attempting to drag himself on again. This time he moved for only a few inches, but he felt that he ought to be close to the saloon wall.

With his cheek pressed to the dirt he looked at the ground ahead. The saloon wasn't before him, so he craned his neck. He found that he'd been dragging himself along beside the saloon and he was no nearer to it than when he'd been shot. Strangely he also felt cooler.

He judged this to be a bad sign and almost gave up trying to move, accepting his fate. Then to his relief he saw that he'd crawled partly beneath a collapsed length of the saloon wall. There was a triangular-shaped gap here, and perhaps a place to hide.

He resumed dragging himself on and after another clawed few inches of movement, he heard talking near by.

'How many were with you?' Hudson Gilmore asked.

'Go to hell,' Marshal Granville Coe said.

A muttered comment sounded followed by a slap then more punches.

'I saw three other men,' someone said.

'So did I,' Hudson said, 'but I want to hear him talk.'

'There are three,' Granville murmured; his tone sounded defeated and to be coming from around twenty feet to Montgomery's left, in the derelict saloon.

It appeared that the marshal had been captured, thus destroying Montgomery's small hope of survival. Still he moved himself, seeking the darkest recess beneath the collapsed wall.

'This one's dead,' someone said out on the road.

'What about that man?'

Heavy footfalls sounded, then a stomping of feet. Three rapid gunshots echoed.

'He sure is dead now. The third one got shot too.'

16

'He was crawling towards the saloon. He can't have gone far.'

Footfalls approached from behind forcing Montgomery to ignore the pain that tore through him with every movement, and drag himself on. It became darker, at least giving him comfort that he was getting deeper into the shadows beneath the collapsed wall, but he doubted he'd be able to stay hidden from a thorough search.

He looked up, then flinched. A hand was stretched out only two feet ahead. He tried to twist and move away from it, but his ribs protested.

He lay still, resigned to his fate until he saw that the hand wasn't moving. When he peered up to the face he looked into closed eyes. Flies buzzed and the reek of death wafted over him.

Montgomery had never seen this man before, but he had a thick moustache and was balding. This matched the description of the man they'd been trying to find and that meant the mission was doomed to end in failure in all ways. On the other hand the rank smell suggested that Edmond Shaffer had lain here for several days, so Hudson might not know his body was here.

That optimistic thought gave Montgomery an idea.

Tortuously he dragged himself on and crawled past the body to reach the corner of the saloon. It looked as if Edmond had also crawled into this

17

shelter to die, but perhaps with luck he might not have to suffer the same fate.

He shuffled round on the spot and dragged his feet until they were placed against Edmond's chest. His legs were still numb, but with a hand braced against the collapsed wall he shoved.

The body rolled over to land on its front with a heavy thud; luckily it dislodged a plank of wood that had been leaning against the saloon wall. On the road someone shouted about the noise and a few moments later gunfire tore out, making Edmond's jacket fray accompanied by punching sounds.

The shots didn't move the body, but Montgomery hoped that in the poor light the shooter wouldn't be able to see its decaying state, nor his own form. To his delight a cry of triumph sounded.

'That's the last of them!' the shooter declared.

'Except for this one,' Hudson Gilmore said, 'who'll now talk if he wants to live.'

Scuffling sounded along with several thuds of fist on flesh.

Montgomery could imagine what was happening in the saloon, but, having escaped seemingly certain death, he was unsure how he could use his presumed demise to help the marshal.

He rolled over on to his back and for the first time he appraised the damage. Blood soaked the jacket above his right hip and below his ribs. He couldn't bring himself to move the jacket aside, but he was sure that unless he got help quickly, his death would no longer remain mistakenly presumed.

His quick examination also showed him that he had dropped his gun. So, feeling even less confident of being able to do anything to help Granville, he sought a gap in the saloon wall through which to look inside. When he found one he watched proceedings for only a few seconds before his disgust forced him to move away.

Granville had been strung up in a corner of the derelict saloon, his hands above his head and tied to a protruding beam that forced him to stand on tiptoe. Hudson Gilmore was pacing back and forth before him, fingering a long, curved knife. The other five men had taken up positions around the room.

'What do you want me to say?' Granville said with a catch in his voice that showed he had already been browbeaten into submission.

'I don't know,' Hudson said. 'Tell me something that'll help me and maybe I'll let you live.'

Someone muttered a comment that generated a round of laughter. So despite his reluctance to watch, Montgomery raised himself again to look into the room. This time he was so weak he could barely lift his head to the gap.

In the saloon Granville was watching as Hudson stopped pacing. His eyes were wide with terror and Montgomery couldn't blame him. Granville was a determined lawman, but few men could remain calm

19

in a hopeless situation like this.

Hudson raised the knife, letting it catch the rays of the high sun and reflect them into Granville's eyes, forcing him to look away. When he looked back Hudson had moved in. He ripped open the front of Granville's vest and laid the flat of the blade against his chest, making him flinch.

Granville looked down at the blade and then looked at Hudson. He gulped.

'All right,' he breathed. 'Come closer and I'll talk.'

Hudson leaned towards him and Granville's mouth moved, whispering something. The brief statement was uttered in a tone too low for Montgomery to hear what was said, and Hudson's men glanced at each other, clearly not having heard the marshal either, but his words made Hudson nod.

'Obliged,' he said. 'Now you can enjoy the knife.'

Granville's mouth fell open as if in surprise that his statement hadn't saved him, before he got his wits about him.

'You double-crosser,' he muttered.

Hudson placed the knife sideways then slipped it towards Granville's mouth. Granville jerked his head away, but when Hudson tracked his movement with the blade he caught on to what Hudson's intention was and he clamped his teeth around the knife.

Hudson backed away leaving Granville with a knife he could use to free himself, albeit only with extreme difficulty. Then he turned to his men.

'We ride!' Hudson called with an overhead gesture as he paced out of the saloon.

'Are we really leaving him?' someone asked. 'He could come after us.'

Hudson stopped at the edge of Montgomery's vision.

'I always honour my deals,' he said. He turned with a smirk on his face and considered the hopeful-looking Granville. 'Except I don't always get thanked.'

Hudson turned on the spot, looking beyond the saloon's short walls at the abandoned town. Then he mimed the gesture of striking a match, which made his men laugh.

Quickly two men gathered a pile of wood, after which another man moved in with an armful of tumbleweed for kindling. This man set fire to the tinder-dry pile, which gathered flames within seconds. Then, using a brand, he moved on to torch first the short wall beside the entrance and then the full-length wall behind Granville.

Within a minute the flames found a welcome home.

As Granville struggled against his bonds, seeking to free himself before the fire could spread, Montgomery gave up on his fight to keep his head raised and he dropped down to lie on the ground.

Crackling sounded as the fire that would surely burn the abandoned town to the ground took hold.

21

But he was too weak for the thought of being burnt alive to trouble him.

Darkness came.

CHAPTER 3

'We've got trouble,' Ryan O'Donnell said when he reached the porch.

Alexander was chopping wood at the back of their house, so he hurried round to the front. He batted away the sawdust he'd used to help his grip, then stood with his hands on hips, showing his brother that he'd been caught in the midst of an important activity.

'I've not got the time for trouble today,' he said. 'There's wood to be chopped.'

'There is, and I said I'd deal with it when I'm free.'

'You've said that every day for the last week since Sheriff Pilgrim made you his deputy.' Alexander waited until Ryan frowned before he smiled and gestured for him to join him in sitting on the porch. 'What's today's trouble?'

'This time it's serious.' Ryan gave Alexander a long stare, presumably to warn him about what was to come, so Alexander removed his smile and leaned forward. 'Our father's been seen in Sumner Point. It's thought he's heading this way.'

Alexander blew out his cheeks and leaned back in his chair. He looked across the plains towards Prospect Creek while Ryan searched the horizon giving the impression that he feared Casey O'Donnell might come riding into view at any moment.

Ryan pointed out a distant tendril of smoke rising up from below the horizon and seeming to be in the direction of Kendall Springs. The brothers cast concerned looks at each other, as if somehow that might be their father's doing, until with a shake of the head Ryan looked away and Alexander sighed.

'How long will it take him to get here?' Alexander asked.

'It depends on how careful he's being, but he was seen skulking around a week ago, so he's had enough time already.'

'If he comes, it'll be hard for me to know what to do for the best, but it'll be impossible for you.'

'It won't. I wasn't a deputy sheriff when he left, but I am now and I know my duty.' Ryan frowned, showing that despite his tough words he was still as perturbed as Alexander was. He lowered his voice. 'But that won't mean I'll feel pleased with myself.'

'I know. Life's been improving recently, so I reckon it'll be best for everyone if he goes somewhere else.'

Ryan nodded, but he didn't speak again for a while as both brothers pondered on what their wayward father's reasons for returning could be.

Since he'd disappeared information had been sparse and contradictory on where he'd been and what he'd done. Then again, information on his activities had always been slow to reach them, and then it had usually been shrouded in mystery.

Throughout their childhood Casey had committed numerous petty crimes while spending more time away from home on unspecified, but no doubt felonious, activities than he'd spent with them. Casey's defence of his behaviour was that his thieving had been for small amounts and that he'd never killed anyone.

Ryan and Alexander's only comfort was that he'd rarely gained from his illegal activities as he was always getting caught.

His absences meant that their long-suffering mother had had the most influence on them and they had never felt an urge to emulate him. But after their mother died he'd returned to look after them as best a man could when he was as useless at being a thief as he was at being a father. Unfortunately that meant he had then become involved in most of the trouble that had happened in the expanding town.

As the brothers grew old enough to understand and abhor the wrong he was doing, frequent arguments developed. Later these had grown in ferocity

25

until one day he'd skulked away without explanation.

The brothers had hoped they wouldn't see or hear about him again. But a few weeks later Casey achieved lasting infamy when in spectacular fashion he escalated his criminal activities from his usual petty thieving.

Outside the nearby town of Kendall Springs he and three other lowlifes carried out a daring raid on the railroad payroll that had passed through Prospect Creek on its way to Sumner Point.

As they'd stolen $10,000, Sheriff Harris and his posse, together with railroad men and bounty hunters, had frantically searched for them. With dozens of men in pursuit the raiders were chased over the state line and for weeks they were hounded until the news died out about their movements.

Despite the lack of developments, for months afterwards the raid and the failed pursuit had been the only talking point in town.

As nobody knew the names of the other three raiders, by default Casey had became known as the ringleader and so Alexander's and Ryan's reputations had suffered. For a year dark mutterings and suspicious glares followed them everywhere until the incident in the Horned Moon last week when Ryan had saved Edmond Shaffer's life.

Since then it appeared that people were prepared to accept them as a part of the community again.

The stolen payroll had never been recovered.

'Do you hope he'll stay one step ahead of me and the rest of the law?' Ryan asked.

'No,' Alexander said without thinking. 'Having an infamous outlaw for a father is bad enough, but having a brother who failed to catch an outlaw would be worse.'

Ryan nodded, then rose to his feet. 'I'll see what else I can find out.'

'Yeah, and hopefully all the wood will be cut when you return.'

Ryan gave his brother a supportive smile. 'There'll be some tough times ahead. I'll do my share when they're over.'

The brothers nodded to each other. Then Ryan headed to his horse and hurried back to town.

Alexander stood on the porch watching him leave. When he'd disappeared into the distance he tried to pick out the thin plume of smoke again, but the light had changed and this time he couldn't see it. Then, instead of returning to the back of the house to continue with the chopping, he slipped inside.

He stood in their small three-room house for a minute, trying to force himself to feel an emotion that would tell him if he were annoyed, worried or perhaps even elated. But he felt numb, so he went to the door to his room.

'He's gone,' he said, opening the door a fraction. 'You can come out now.'

The door opened and furtive eyes glanced around

27

the room before a man emerged. He was greying at the temples, his physique was wiry and weathered.

'Obliged, son,' he said.

Montgomery Pierce's feet were getting warmer.

He stretched, enjoying the feeling, but his skin continued to heat up and with a shocked murmur he became fully awake and recalled his predicament.

Despite his desperate situation time had passed since Hudson Gilmore had torched the town. Now smoke billowed past him and flames crackled close by.

He forced himself away from the heat, but that sent a bolt of pain thrusting through his wounded side and, worse, he moved into a patch of thicker smoke. Not knowing which route would be the safest, he stopped and forced himself to think.

The smoke was moving quickly and he decided to head with it in the hope that it was being funnelled through a large gap in the wall. He coughed weakly, then held his breath as he moved on.

His gamble paid off when after clawing along for a few feet he reached a position where he could clamber into the saloon, if he could summon the strength.

Granville was the only one left inside and he was twisting and shaking, trying to free himself from the rope that secured him to the beam above his head. Montgomery judged that he'd be unlikely to succeed and neither could he see the knife Hudson had left.

He called out, but his voice emerged as a strangulated cough and he failed to attract Granville's
attention. So he gritted his teeth, then rolled over to
land on the saloon floor. After accomplishing that
manoeuvre with greater ease than he'd expected,
like a sidewinder he snaked across the floor towards
Granville.

As he became cooler, he saw more of the saloon
and surroundings. Flames were licking at the walls
and as the roof had gone he could see that the sky
was thick with black smoke as the rest of the town
burned. There was no sign of Hudson Gilmore and
his men.

'Is that you, Montgomery?' Granville called.

Montgomery stopped crawling to look at
Granville. To his delight he found that he'd dragged
himself halfway across the saloon floor.

'Yeah,' he murmured, 'just.'

'I want to hear about how you survived, but later.'

Montgomery nodded, then resumed snaking his
way along until he reached Granville's feet. When he
stopped to consider his next actions he saw the knife,
which Granville had dropped. He clamped a hand
on it, then jabbed the point down into the wood and
used it to lever himself up to a sitting position.

His side was burning with pain, but by favouring it
he'd been able to cross the floor. So, after flexing his
legs and making the knees and ankles bend, he reck-

oned he could stand up. He just had to think through the actions beforehand. So in his mind he rehearsed moving to one knee, then to a crouching position and then standing.

Sadly that activity felt too strenuous. It was warm and sleep was more appealing. Fascinating shapes were rippling along the shiny blade. They were tinged with red.

He closed his eyes. . . .

Granville kicked his legs. Montgomery shooed him away, but the marshal wouldn't stop hitting him.

Montgomery opened his eyes to find he was lying down again with the knife thrust point down into the wooden floor inches from his face. It was flickering with the reflected flames.

'What the. . . ?' he murmured.

'You passed out!' Granville shouted. 'You have to stay awake. Just free me. I'll do the rest.'

Montgomery nodded, but he still didn't move and oblivion was again beckoning him. He shook himself, gathering a moment of clarity when he accepted that he had to force himself to move or he'd rest here for ever.

He hunched his shoulders, then pressed down on the knife and shoved himself up to his knees. His ribs protested with every inch he raised himself, but when he settled down the pain receded. Worryingly this position let him see that all the walls were now fully ablaze and flames were gaining a hold on the wooden floor, which would be impregnated with years of spilt liquor.

He now felt as hot as he had been when he'd lain beneath the collapsed wall. So he took a deep breath and with Granville shouting encouragement he clutched his stomach, as if that could contain the pain, then went to one knee with his left leg raised ready to stand.

Something in his chest tore and a fresh wave of dampness dribbled through his fingers. He couldn't help but cry out and while he continued to shriek he put his weight on his left leg and dragged his right leg up until he was standing.

He staggered around on the spot, but as he reckoned he wouldn't get up again if he fell, he fought to stay on his feet.

'I did it,' he said through clenched teeth when he'd stopped moving. Even better, he still held the knife.

Still doubled over he side-stepped towards Granville until he walked into him and Granville helped him by remaining rigid.

'Raise the knife and cut the rope,' Granville said, his voice strained. Then he coughed as a thick plume of smoke blew over them.

Montgomery didn't reckon he could remain standing if he started coughing, so he held his breath and forced his head up. He gained a more upright position than he'd expected to manage, then clamped the hand that had been holding his stomach on Granville's shoulder. He eyed the rope above Granville's head and swung the knife up to meet it.

The blade was sharp and it cut into the rope, but the rope also moved away from him, forcing him to stretch to put pressure on it. With his weight pressing against Granville's chest they teetered backwards for a pace. That at least made the rope tighten, and the knife cut into it more readily.

Montgomery swayed as waves of hot agony writhed through his ribs, but the movement helped him to produce a sawing motion.

'Just a few more cuts,' Montgomery muttered, talking to take his mind off the throbbing pain that was now spreading to his whole body.

'Keep going,' Granville said. He stared into Montgomery's eyes as if he could give him strength through eye contact alone. 'Then we'll both live.'

'Talk to me,' Montgomery said, his teeth gritted. 'Tell me what you told Hudson to spare your life.'

'It didn't work. He left me here to die.'

'Not yet.' Montgomery sawed twice more, cutting through to the last few taut lengths of twine, but then his strength gave out and he lowered the knife. 'It looked like you gave him a place and a name.'

Granville didn't reply, so Montgomery thought back, letting the memory distract him from the pain so that he could raise the knife again. He just needed to make one more strong slice to part the rope.

As the memory consumed him, the knife rose to the rope. He remembered Granville mouthing a place that had looked like Prospect Creek and then a name like Billy Hopwell or perhaps. . . .

The knife bit deep and the rope parted. For a moment both men stood in their stretched out positions. Then they keeled over.

Granville broke Montgomery's fall, but his collapse to the floor gave him such a sick feeling in the guts that he couldn't bring himself to move to find out how badly he'd been hurt. He was vaguely aware of Granville dragging himself out from under him and then of him shuffling around as he presumably freed the rope from his wrists.

Blackness came, interspersed with flickering red light and brief muffled sounds. The noise could have been Granville talking to him, but he couldn't force his mind to dwell on what he was saying.

Then he felt as if he was alone.

The feeling became stronger, so he forced his eyes open. His gaze focused on a pair of boots ten feet away and he raised his gaze from them up to Granville's face.

Granville had a kerchief over his mouth and behind him were rising flames. His eyes widened, suggesting he was smiling.

'You saved my life,' he said. 'I won't ever forget that.'

He turned and headed towards the flames. He stopped with an arm raised before his face, clearly working out his best option. Then a gust of wind parted the wall of fire and he slipped through the gap to leave the saloon.

Lying on his side Montgomery watched the flames spread to fill the gap. Then he waited for Granville to return.

The fire grew brighter and hotter, drying the sweat from his face to leave him feeling like a baked husk, but Granville didn't reappear. So instead Montgomery watched the flames dance across the saloon floor.

He closed his eyes before they reached him.

CHAPTER 4

'They say your good-for-nothing father's heading this way,' Frank Buchanan said.

Ryan O'Donnell stayed hunched over at the bar and took deep breaths. Earlier, with Sheriff Pilgrim being engaged in a private and heated conversation with a visiting US marshal in the sheriff's office, he'd backtracked out of the office rapidly. He'd decided he shouldn't hide himself away, so he'd come to the Horned Moon and although he'd feared he'd get this reaction, he'd not worked out how he should deal with it.

With a resigned sigh he turned to Frank. He was pleased to see that the customers in the packed saloon room were looking at his tormentor with irritation. Heartened he kept his voice level.

'I've heard, but he has no reason to come here.'

Frank ground his jaw, his narrowed eyes showing that he was running various retorts through his mind, searching for the right thing to say to provoke an argument.

'Except to give his sons their cut of the railroad payroll.'

'We're honest men,' Ryan muttered. 'Everyone knows that.'

Frank looked around for support, but he received only shaken heads and murmured requests to quieten.

'I guess we'll find out soon enough if his family care more for him than they do for this town.'

The saloon room quietened as everyone awaited Ryan's response and Ryan couldn't blame them. If he were an uninvolved bystander in this situation, he would wonder the same. So when he replied he turned on the spot to address everyone in the room rather than just Frank.

'You can't choose your family,' he proclaimed, 'but you can choose your friends. I hate one member of the former. I respect all of the latter.'

Ryan had meant to say more, but even before he'd finished speaking his statement had gathered several supportive comments. Then two customers moved over to persuade Frank to desist. Ryan turned back to the bar.

'No matter how important you reckon you've become since Foster Pilgrim made you his deputy,' Frank said, ignoring the prevailing mood in the saloon, 'you'll always have an outlaw for a father.'

Ryan was still deciding whether to ignore him or retort when Sheriff Pilgrim came in and headed across the room to join him. Everyone fell silent.

The lawman whom Ryan had seen in the law office followed him in and Pilgrim introduced him as US Marshal Granville Coe. His low tone suggested that worrying news was to come.

When Pilgrim stood back to let Granville speak, the marshal acknowledged Ryan with a quick nod. Then he faced the customers. He took a whiskey glass from the bar and banged it down three times, although he already had everyone's attention.

'I'm looking to recruit special deputies for an important mission,' he said.

'Don't worry,' Frank said, glaring at Ryan. 'We're already on the lookout for the outlaw Casey O'Donnell.'

'I'm pleased you already know about him.' Granville looked around the saloon. 'So whether you join me or not, you all need to report any sightings.'

The customers murmured that they'd do this, although several men cast embarrassed glances at Ryan.

Pilgrim had his jaw set firm. Ryan had worked with him for only a week, but that was long enough to gather that he sympathized with how difficult this was for him and that he'd brought Granville to the saloon only reluctantly.

'I'll join you,' Frank said loudly. 'I'm always eager

to shoot up low-down snakes.'

Frank walked past Ryan while licking his lips with relish for the task ahead. Ryan ignored him, figuring that if Frank were to ride off with the marshal he wouldn't need to answer his accusations.

When Frank had swung round to stand beside him Granville slapped his shoulder. Then he waited for this first acceptance to encourage others to join him, but proving how out of line Frank was with everyone else's attitude, the other customers didn't meet the marshal's eye.

'I know you have mixed feelings about Casey,' Granville said when it became clear that nobody else would volunteer. 'But you could all be in danger. A railroad man Edmond Shaffer failed to return to Sumner Point. The town marshal suspected foul play and Casey O'Donnell's name came up. As I was already tracking Casey I got called in. I followed the leads to a derelict town out west where I gathered up two bodies along with a badly wounded man.'

Ryan frowned at the news that the man whose life he had saved in this very saloon might be dead. Sheriff Jerry Harris had been killed in that incident. Ryan had killed two of the three gunslingers while Deputy Foster Pilgrim had tracked down and killed the third man. Afterwards Pilgrim had been appointed sheriff and his first act had been to appoint Ryan as his deputy.

Granville glanced at Ryan, perhaps acknowledging

he knew of his feelings on the matter, before he looked at Pilgrim, who stepped forward.

'He means Kendall Springs,' he said. 'Apparently someone burnt down the buildings and now Doctor Tuttle is caring for the man Granville rescued.'

If Granville had hoped this information would galvanize the customers, he was disappointed. Aside from a few people murmuring that the demise of the town was long overdue, nobody said anything.

'Is there,' Granville said, turning to Pilgrim with his face set in a scowl, 'anywhere in town where men gather?'

Pilgrim said nothing, although the insult made several men stand to confront him before they were dragged back down. Frank leaned forward.

'I'll help you,' he said. 'Follow me.'

Granville nodded and after casting an irritated glare around the saloon he followed Frank outside, leaving the customers to make their own explanations to each other as to why they'd refused his offer.

'If he wants to hire men who'll enjoy hunting another man,' Ryan said when Pilgrim had edged along the bar to stand beside him, 'I'd guess he's heading to the Lone Star.'

'He's welcome to anyone he can find in there.' Pilgrim sighed and looked through the window, watching the two men depart. 'But maybe I judged him harshly. I wasn't pleased when he rode into town with a half-dead man and then told me what my priorities are, but perhaps he deserves our support.'

'He does, but I'm not joining him. I'll look out for Casey O'Donnell and I'll do my duty, but I won't ride with Frank Buchanan.'

'I wasn't asking you to.' Pilgrim offered a smile. 'Go to Doctor Tuttle. See if he'll let you question this wounded man. Burning down a town and shooting up a heap of men doesn't sound like something Casey would do. Get a different view on this before Granville rides off with Frank Buchanan and his friends from the Lone Star.'

'I wouldn't wish that on anyone,' Ryan said with a supportive smile. 'Even my father.'

'How do you feel?'

Montgomery Pierce reckoned he'd been asked this question several times, but he hadn't felt strong enough and sufficiently awake to reply before. The only feeling he could muster was relief that Granville had come back for him, after all, but then he registered that the voice wasn't Granville's.

He tried to push himself up, but restraining hands slapped down on his shoulders, urging him to stay put. When he opened his eyes and focused on the man looking down at him he saw that he was no longer in the burning saloon.

'What happened?' he croaked.

The words grated in his throat, causing him almost as much pain as his ribs had. That made him realize that his chest now felt so numb it was if it wasn't there, although whether that was a good sign or a bad one he didn't know.

'You got lucky.'

The man identified himself as Doctor Tuttle. Then in soothing tones he described Montgomery's injuries, which included smoke inhalation, burns, and a bullet wound that had needed plenty of work to clean out then stitch up.

'Will I live?'

'I did my best. You were lucky that Marshal Granville Coe happened across you while you still had enough life left in you, but the wound was serious. You need to rest.'

Montgomery had gathered enough of his senses to know that Tuttle hadn't described his rescue accurately, but it didn't feel as if it was worth the effort that would be required to explain.

'Thank you,' he whispered. Then he looked to the ceiling of the surgery, enjoying the unexpected bonus of somehow surviving the ordeal of his encounter with Hudson Gilmore.

Tuttle moved away, but he stopped in the doorway where he had a brief discussion with someone. Montgomery couldn't hear the words, although he gathered he was being talked about. The debate ended and the man approached.

'You have two minutes,' Tuttle called after the newcomer, 'and don't distress my patient.'

41

The newcomer nodded then sat down beside him, getting into a position where Montgomery could look at him with his cheek resting on the pillow.

'I'm Deputy Ryan O'Donnell,' he said.

'I'm Deputy Montgomery Pierce.' He considered. 'Although I guess I'm just Montgomery again now. I'll be no use to Granville any more as a special deputy.'

'I hadn't realized that. I understood the marshal found you in the burnt-out wreck of a saloon in Kendall Springs.'

Hearing this version of events for a second time made Montgomery shrug, but he presumed that Granville had his reasons.

'It's a long story,' he said, speaking low with an exaggerated weakness to give himself time to work out how he should react. But the talking made him cough and by the time he'd managed to control himself he felt weaker.

'I'll cut to the basics. Did you get into a gunfight with Casey O'Donnell?' Ryan waited but Montgomery was still struggling to make his throat work properly, so Ryan continued: 'He could be coming here, so Granville's trying to recruit special deputies to catch him.'

'Granville's a good man,' Montgomery gasped, talking in short bursts. 'He was looking for Edmond Shaffer. But Hudson Gilmore shot us up. He saved my life. I trust Granville.'

He wanted to say more, but the long speech was threatening to make him cough again, so he quietened and returned to looking at the ceiling.

'I've heard of Hudson. He used to work for the railroad, but a year ago he led a payroll detail. He and his men got drunk and when they sobered up the money had been stolen. He lost his job.' Ryan stood. 'I'll call in on you later and see how you're doing. We deputies need to watch out for each other.'

Montgomery smiled and watched him head to the door, where he was met by the doctor.

'You learnt enough, Deputy O'Donnell?' Tuttle asked.

'I got what I came for,' Ryan said. He glanced at Montgomery.

For his next comment Ryan lowered his voice to a whisper and although Montgomery couldn't hear the words he was sure Ryan asked if he would live.

Tuttle's pensive smile provided the answer he dreaded: that the matter was still undecided, but it made Montgomery remember the previous occasion when he'd tried to lip-read. He'd not heard what Granville had said to Hudson, but he was sure it had been a place and a name.

After the exertions of the last few minutes his eyes were tired and he would welcome sleep but, as the two men left, he summoned up an image of Granville speaking. He was no longer in a position to use the information, but he owed his life to that statement.

'Go to Prospect Creek and you'll find Billy Hopwell,' he murmured to himself, remembering his guesses.

The town sounded right, but not the name.

'Or maybe Billy Howell or . . . Billy O'Donnell?'

The moment he said the last name his heart thudded and he was sure he was nearly right. He considered again and decided that he'd got the surname right, but not the Christian name.

That had been . . . Casey O'Donnell.

With that mystery solved Montgomery relaxed and let sleep claim him.

CHAPTER 5

'The whole town's edgy now,' Ryan said when he returned home, 'now that this US marshal is on our father's tail.'

Alexander shrugged. 'With any luck all the activity will keep him away.'

Ryan joined him at the table. 'We must hope so for his sake as much as ours, but the good news is, not many people are blaming us, so this might not open up any old wounds.'

Alexander considered him, appearing as if he wanted to say something, but instead he went to the fire and gathered up the cooking-pot containing a thick stew. While pondering Ryan watched him potter around ladling the meal on to plates.

When he moved on to Ryan's plate the ladle missed its target and its contents dribbled on the floor. Then, when he bent to clean it up, he tipped over the plate, which made him frown and back away.

'Where do you reckon he'll go?' Alexander asked, when Ryan moved in to mop up the mess instead.

'I don't know, but he was resourceful enough to remain free despite all the men who were chasing him.' Ryan looked up and winked. 'So relax, it's not as if we need to save any of this stew for him.'

Alexander uttered a snort of laughter, but the sound was strained, proving the situation was making it hard for him to cope. They ate in silence, and when Ryan filled another ladle from the pot Alexander declined the offer of more, and then he didn't finish his meal either.

'I guess I'm not hungry,' he said, pushing his plate away.

They kept a few head of cattle, so when Ryan had finished eating Alexander took the leftover food out to them. Ryan didn't comment on this being a bad idea, but he had to smile when his distracted brother took his plate with him.

Ryan followed him out on to the porch and watched him disappear round the back of their small barn. When he returned he'd left both the pot and the plate.

'You want to head into Prospect Creek this evening?' Ryan asked. When Alexander shook his head he continued: 'Provided you can remember where the town is.'

'I can remember,' Alexander snapped with uncharacteristic anger.

'Hey,' Ryan said, raising his hands. 'I was just trying to break you out of that bad mood.'

He sat down and after a moment's thought Alexander sat beside him and let out a long sigh.

'I'm sorry, but I don't like this situation.'

'Neither do I, but it could go on for weeks, so you need to calm down.' As Alexander didn't reply Ryan watched the cows roam into view beyond the fence, presumably having eaten the leftovers. He pointed at them. 'I'll fetch the pot.'

'I'll get it,' Alexander said, leaping to his feet and showing more animation than he had done at any other time this evening.

He hurried on and was halfway to the barn before Ryan could get out of his chair. Ryan got to his feet and with his hands on his hips he went on a slow stroll after him.

'What's worrying you?' he asked when Alexander emerged from round the side of the building.

'Nothing other than Casey,' Alexander said, heading past him.

Ryan decided not to press the issue and he carried on towards the fence, aiming to give him some space, but Alexander doubled back and stood before him, blocking his way.

The two brothers looked at each other. Alexander was the first to look away and Ryan couldn't help but notice he'd brought the pot back but not the plate.

'Something's wrong,' Ryan said. When Alexander

47

didn't reply he patted his shoulder. 'But you can tell me about it in your own time.'

He moved to side-step round Alexander, but Alexander followed his movement before he checked himself and let his brother pass. Ryan's heart thudded as a worrying thought hit him and at that moment, from the corner of his eye, he saw a shadow flitter beyond the partly open barn door.

Ryan closed his eyes and offered a silent prayer that he was wrong. Then he set off for the barn. Alexander didn't follow, so at the door Ryan stopped and looked at him.

'Don't,' Alexander said.

'Just talk to me,' Ryan said.

Alexander only lowered his head, so Ryan slipped inside. In the darkened interior he cast his slow gaze around the barn while hoping he was wrong and that another explanation for Alexander's odd behaviour would materialize.

He completed his consideration without noticing anything untoward, which allowed him to breathe more easily, but he still threw open the doors to provide more light. He'd taken two steady paces forward when he noticed the shiny edge of Alexander's plate poking out from behind a pile of hay. He looked to the roof, sighed, then backed away to the door and bade Alexander to approach.

'I'm sorry,' Alexander murmured when he joined him. 'I didn't want you to know.'

'Why did you think you could keep him hidden in a house this size?'

'I was working on a plan to get him away. I just needed another day.'

'And that would have made it all right, would it?'

Alexander frowned, acknowledging that in this situation nothing he could say would placate his brother, and so it was left for the subject of their argument to speak up.

'I should have realized,' Casey said from the back of the barn, 'that I wouldn't get a good reception from you.'

Ryan took his time in turning and facing a man he'd never wanted to see again. His father hadn't changed much in the last year. He'd always looked to be in need of a meal and the eyes were just as furtive.

'Casey O'Donnell,' Ryan said with due gravity, 'you're under arrest.'

'Arrest?' Casey spluttered, glancing past him at Alexander, but what he saw there didn't cheer him. 'What makes you think you can do that, Ryan?'

'That's Deputy Sheriff Ryan O'Donnell.' Ryan set his feet wide apart. 'You can either come voluntarily, be tied up, or be shot. It's your choice.'

Casey raised a hand while taking a backward pace.

'Now, hold on a minute there, son. You have to hear my story first.'

'You have the right to explain yourself, but you can do it from the inside of a cell,' Ryan said, taking a

49

pace forward, 'just like all outlaws can.'

'I'm not going in no cell.'

Ryan had left his six-shooter back in the house. He turned, but Alexander spread his arms, encouraging him to stay.

'Listen to him,' he said.

Ryan shook his head. 'Nothing he can say will make me change my mind.'

Alexander shrugged. 'So what have you got to lose by listening?'

Ryan couldn't think of a retort, so with a sigh he turned back to find that Casey had sidled along the side of the barn to reach the door. His darting gaze suggested he was weighing up his chances of running.

'Tell me your story quickly,' Ryan said. 'Then I'll take you into town.'

'I'm guilty of doing plenty of things, Ryan,' Casey said. He spread his hands. 'But I didn't carry out that payroll robbery.'

'How can I believe that? Everyone knows it was you.'

'You know the kind of crimes I committed. Do you reckon I could have pulled off a raid like that?' Casey spread his arms and looked down, drawing Ryan's attention to his dishevelled state. 'Do I look as if I have ten thousand dollars?'

Ryan sighed. 'I guess not. You look like hell.'

'Then I look like I feel.' Casey raised his hat to run

fingers through his sparse hair. 'Before I came here I did something I'm not proud of.'

Ryan waited for more details, but when they weren't forthcoming he considered. Although he didn't want to, he had to admit that his father's tone had sounded honest and that he did appear as if he wanted to confess about his activities, whether those details were to his advantage or not.

He lowered his head in resignation, then gestured to the house, but he set off first to ensure he got to his gun before Casey could. Casey joined Alexander and they followed him while talking in low and urgent tones. Ryan continued on to the house, only stopping and turning on reaching the door.

He winced when he saw what they had been talking about. A line of riders was approaching, coming from the opposite direction to Prospect Creek. They were a half-mile away and they were riding quickly enough to reach the house within a few minutes.

Ryan beckoned for Alexander and Casey to hurry on and join him. Without questioning him Casey slipped into the shadows on the porch while Alexander glared at Ryan with one foot placed up on a chair.

'It's time for you to decide, Ryan,' he said, regaining his usual quiet authority as he leaned on his knee, 'whether duty is more important than family.'

'I already have.' Ryan turned to Casey. 'I'll make

THE SONS OF CASEY O'DONNELL

sure you get to tell your story, but you won't do it as a free man.'

Casey sneered. 'Then I no longer have a son.'

Casey stepped up to him and raised a hand to thrust him aside before going into the house.

In response Ryan grabbed his arm. Then using a ploy he'd perfected during a saloon-room fight that had broken out shortly after he'd become a deputy, he bent the arm while using Casey's momentum to drag him forward and twist him round.

A moment later Casey found himself held from behind with his arm thrust so far up his back he would hurt himself if he tried to get free. He still struggled, but on finding that Ryan had a firm grip he looked at Alexander.

'And it's time for you to decide, Alexander,' Casey said, 'whether family is more important than duty.'

To Ryan's irritation Alexander didn't react other than to stare at the subdued Casey, then at the approaching riders. They were still at least two minutes away. He frowned then gave a brief nod before he walked past Ryan and into the house.

'If you've got something to say,' Ryan said into Casey's ear, 'say it now before Sheriff Pilgrim gets here.'

'I've got nothing to say to no lawman. I'll only speak to my son.'

Casey's tone was more confident than one would expect from a man who was about to see his liberty removed permanently. Ryan tried to dismiss the flurry of doubt that rippled in his stomach and when he sensed Alexander stepping up to him from behind he forced himself to keep looking forward.

'Keep the gun on him, Alexander,' he said, 'and this will be over soon.'

'Can't do that, Ryan,' Alexander said, using a heavy tone that made Casey snort with approval.

'You can.' Ryan kept his voice level, not wanting to entertain the possibility that Alexander was planning to defy him. 'Do what I said and we won't speak of this again.'

Alexander moved forward to look at the riders, letting Ryan see that he had brought his six-shooter. He was keeping it lowered, but as he wouldn't meet Ryan's eye what was going through his mind was obvious.

'You have to trust me,' he said. 'You aren't taking him to jail, but he can't get away before those men arrive either. As we're standing in the shadows, they might not have seen him, so we'll hide him.'

Ryan shook his head. 'I won't lie to you. I won't go along with that plan. This ends before Sheriff Pilgrim arrives.'

Alexander opened his mouth to snap back a response, but Casey spoke up first.

'Stop standing around arguing, you two,' he urged. He nodded towards the riders. 'That's no lawman approaching.'

53

Ryan looked at the advancing riders with narrowed eyes. They were close enough for him to discern six men.

He couldn't see their faces yet, but the lead man was riding ahead confidently.

'Who is he?' he asked.

'That's Hudson Gilmore. And that means only one of us will get to leave here alive.'

CHAPTER 6

'Is the situation really that bad?' Alexander asked, and when Ryan nodded he swung round to Casey. 'I said I'd help you, but I'm not getting stuck in the middle of an argument with your outlaw friends.'

'Hudson Gilmore's no friend of mine,' Casey said. 'But he's no outlaw.'

'He's the railroad man who was supposed to be guarding the payroll Pa stole,' Ryan said. He raised a hand when Casey bristled and started to say he hadn't stolen it. 'After it went missing, I heard he'd fallen on bad times.'

'Then he's not coming here to be friendly,' Alexander said casting Casey a harsh glare, but with the limited time remaining before Hudson arrived he didn't press for more details.

Ryan manoeuvred his father into the house, then released him and shoved him forward. Alexander followed them in and hurried to his room. He emerged quickly with all the weaponry they had: two more six-shooters along with a box of bullets.

'Despite everything,' Ryan said, 'we can't let Hudson have him.'

'I know,' Alexander said holding out the weapons. 'But we two can't do that alone. We have to put aside our differences so that we can all join forces to defend ourselves.'

For long moments he and Ryan looked at each other until Ryan gave a reluctant nod.

'He gets a gun,' he said, 'but I take the lead and I'll try to stop this situation getting out of control. The moment this is over he turns over his gun.'

Throughout his declaration he hadn't looked at Casey, so it was left for Alexander to face their father and draw forth a grunt of agreement. Casey had sounded uncommitted, so Alexander didn't hand over the gun immediately, but the sounds of the riders drawing up outside added urgency to the situation.

With a heavy sigh Alexander handed a gun to Casey and then passed the last one to Ryan.

Ryan went to a window. Outside, the six men were dismounting beside the barn calmly, although Hudson gestured to two men to take up positions on either side of the barn and for one other to get inside it, where he knelt down beside the doors. Hudson and the rest faced the house.

'I've come for Casey O'Donnell,' he declared.

56

'Send him out and we'll leave.'

None of the men outside had drawn their guns, so with a gesture to the others to stay out of sight, Ryan opened the door, but he stayed in the doorway.

'Who are you,' he said, 'to give orders to a deputy sheriff?'

'I'm Hudson Gilmore. You'll have heard of me.'

'Sure. I heard you lost your job.' Ryan suppressed a smile when Hudson firmed his jaw in irritation. 'But you can rest assured that Casey will be dealt with. He's under arrest.'

'You expect me to believe that his own son has arrested him?'

Ryan hadn't given Hudson his name.

'That's no concern of mine. Now get off my land or I'll arrest you next.'

Hudson smiled, then drew Ryan's attention to the number of men who were with him. Accordingly these men snorted a burst of confident laughter. Hudson let the light mood run its course until with a wave he gestured at them to stay quiet.

He pointed at Ryan, but he didn't get to utter his threat.

Shuffling sounded within the house, then Casey moved into the window to the left of the door, brandishing his six-shooter. Alexander muttered at him to stay down, but he was too slow to stop him acting. Two rapid shots pealed out.

Presumably Casey had aimed at Hudson and

although his burst of gunfire missed him, one shot hit the man standing to his right, in the upper arm. Before he could fire again Hudson and the others ran for the barn, while the men who were already in attacking positions drew their guns and peppered lead at the house.

Ryan beat a hasty retreat to find that inside Alexander was remonstrating with their father, but Casey was ignoring him as he stayed down and chose his moment to return fire.

Alexander looked at Ryan, who had to bite his lip to avoid making the obvious comment that this was the sort of disaster he'd expected after Alexander had sided with their father. Instead he put his mind to working out how they would prevail.

He headed to the window to the right of the door and risked a glance outside. The barn was the only cover and Hudson and his men had taken refuge there. The wounded man wasn't visible so presumably he'd gone with them.

The two windows and the door were the only ways into the house so they would be able to make it hard for Hudson to get to them. They were four miles out of town but other homesteads being near by, it wouldn't be long before others came to investigate, so they just had to keep their wits about them and be defensive while Hudson took all the risks.

Ryan was about to tell the others his optimistic opinion when Casey blasted off a volley of shots at the barn that attracted further retaliation. As the three men went to their knees, slugs slammed into the outside walls and a few stray shots pinged inside.

Ryan exchanged an exasperated glance with Alexander.

'No more shooting,' Alexander said when the volley of gunfire petered out. 'We could be here for hours.'

'You two can stay here for as long as you like,' Casey snapped. 'I need to see off Hudson, then get away.'

'You're not leaving,' Ryan said.

Casey snapped back an angry oath, but Ryan didn't reply, figuring that they could resolve this battle later as right now they couldn't afford to fight amongst themselves. Instead he looked outside where all was quiet.

For the next five minutes the stand-off didn't develop: none of Hudson's men showing themselves.

Casey shouted taunts, but he got no response, making him even edgier. He moved from window to window to get different angles on the situation and he ignored all demands to calm down. Ryan wouldn't have been surprised if he'd burst out of the door and made a run for a horse.

As it turned out Hudson made the first move.

Rapid gunfire exploded from the barn, forcing the three men in the house to duck down. The gunfire rattled continuously, suggesting that Hudson

59

was using it as cover while his men got into positions closer to the house, but the defenders could do nothing about it.

After a minute the shooting halted; the suddenness of its stopping suggested it was planned and, after casting worried glances at each other, the three men looked out. Ryan couldn't see anyone.

He presumed the men in the barn had all found gaps in the wood through which to fire, but before he could start to pinpoint them a slug whined off the shutters beside his head, forcing him to jerk away.

Alexander and Casey reported that they hadn't seen anyone, but Ryan had no doubt that Hudson had done something. He craned his neck looking along the porch. Nobody was visible, suggesting that if someone had made a run for the house they'd gone to ground round the side.

Long moments passed in silence. Then a clattering sounded at the back of the house.

'There's no way in at the back, is there?' Casey asked.

'We haven't changed the house since you left,' Alexander said using a guarded tone as he listened to another clatter, this time clearly coming from the left of the house. 'Except. . . .'

He ran for the internal door nearest the noise. Ryan kept half an eye on him while still looking outside judging that no matter what the men outside were trying to do they couldn't break in. Then he winced, having had the same concern that had probably worried Alexander.

For the last month he'd been meaning to mend the leaky roof in his room. The men could have climbed on the roof and be seeking to widen the hole.

'Keep watch,' he said to Casey, the urgency of the situation making it easy for him to bite back his distaste at accepting his help.

He hurried across the room to join Alexander where they stood to either side of the door. On the count of three Alexander swung the door open and moved to go in, but a gunshot tore splinters from the door, forcing him to back away.

At that moment gunfire erupted outside as Hudson sought to press home his advantage. With a gleeful grunt Casey started firing at the barn.

'Got one,' he shouted on his third shot, the declaration stopping the firing at the house.

Heartened Ryan and Alexander again tried to move into the doorway.

A quick shot made them back away, but during his brief sight of his room Ryan saw that the attackers had made a large hole in the roof. One man was crouching down on the roof while seeking out the safest way to drop down while a second man covered him. A moment later a thud sounded as the man landed.

In this situation the man who had jumped was at

his most vulnerable; Ryan thrust his hand into the room while keeping himself hidden and sprayed wild gunfire around.

A cry of pain brought him his reward, although when Alexander took over and tried the same tactic he managed only one shot before sustained gunfire tore out, forcing him to back away. Then a second thud sounded as the other man dropped down into the house.

Again the shooting encouraged another volley of shots at the house from the barn, but this time Casey didn't return fire.

Ryan swung round, planning to remonstrate with him, but Casey was standing with his back to the wall looking aloft, his expression defeated and tired. Suddenly he looked his age and for the first time Ryan had to fight down a twinge of compassion for his predicament.

'I won't let Hudson Gilmore get you,' he said.

Casey shrugged. 'Are you speaking as a son or as a lawman?'

'You're an outlaw. . . .' Ryan sighed and spread his hands. 'And you're my father.'

'So the sons of Casey O'Donnell are fighting on the same side as their father at last, are they?'

In the room behind someone whispered a question. The weak groan he received in reply suggested they had wounded one of the attackers, after all. Ryan reckoned he could take care of the other man, so he gestured at Alexander to go to the other window.

'If that's important to you,' Ryan said, 'then they are.'

'In that case when we get out of this, you need to fight for me again, but carefully. I lost one son over that payroll raid and I don't want it to happen again.'

'Sons,' Alexander murmured, but Casey winced as if that wasn't what he meant.

Ryan dismissed the matter with a shrug.

'Are you still claiming,' he said, 'that you should-n't be treated as an outlaw?'

'I know you won't believe me until you see the proof for yourself and I can't blame you. The first I knew of the raid was when I was sitting in a saloon in Sumner Point with three other men. A railroad man pointed us out to the town marshal and he tried to arrest us. We fled, but the others blamed me, reck-oning I had been involved. I've returned to put that right, except I haven't done it well so far, so you need to make sure the truth comes out.'

Ryan considered. 'This man who identified you, would he be Edmond Shaffer?'

'He would,' Casey said with a smile.

'In that case we fight our way out of this mess. Then we talk about it.'

Casey frowned looking as if he wanted to say more, but over by the other window Alexander got his attention with a sorry shake of the head.

'I've seen what he's seen,' he said. 'And we won't get the chance. Another group of men has arrived. We'll never fight them all off.'

Casey looked down at the floor and after a moment he gave a brief nod, as if he'd made a decision. Then he ducked down and scurried along below the window to stand by the door.

'Then I'll give them what they want.' He glanced at both his sons, then with a deep breath he reached for the door.

'Don't,' Ryan said.

'You're the lawman. You've got all the information you need to work this out, and besides, Hudson wants answers before he kills me.' Casey smiled at Ryan, then at Alexander before he shouted through the door. 'I'm coming out, Hudson. Back off and leave the others alone. They have nothing to do with this.'

Casey counted down from three, then raised his hands. He kicked the door open and swung into the doorway. With his steady gaze he surveyed the scene, then stepped forward.

'Get back in!' Alexander shouted, but he was too late.

A moment later a prolonged volley of gunshots tore along the length of the building.

Two heavy footfalls sounded. Then Casey staggered back into the house. He held on to the doorframe, his eyes pained and his chest bloodied, but he couldn't keep himself upright and he slid to the floor.

The men in the back room chose that moment to make their move and scampering footfalls sounded coming towards the door. Ryan ducked down, then went into the room crouching low.

His action saved him from a high shot that winged over his shoulder. Then, before the shooter could get him in his sights, Ryan blasted a slug into his chest that made him drop to the floor.

He looked for the second man, finding him propped up against the back wall. He had a pained expression on his face, one hand was clasped to a bloodied shoulder, the other, shaking, was holding his gun.

Ryan didn't give him a chance to fire; he tore a shot into his chest. The man fell sideways to lie slumped on the floor. After checking that the first man was still and that nobody was on the other side of the hole in the roof, Ryan hurried back into the main room.

Alexander was moving away from the prone form of his father to take up a position by the door, where he caught Ryan's eye. Ryan raised an eyebrow, but Alexander returned a slow shake of the head.

Despite everything Ryan winced.

'If Hudson didn't want to take him alive,' he said, 'what chance do we have?'

'None. They're all moving in.'

Ryan hurried to the window. Alexander had been right. Men were swarming everywhere. He moved back out of view to reload.

'Did he say anything more about the payroll raid?'

'Yeah,' Alexander murmured with a gulp. 'If we live, I'll tell you about it.'

Ryan nodded. Then with a deep breath he moved his gun up on to the sill. He picked out as his target the nearest moving man, but then he stayed his fire.

The man was now close enough for Ryan to recognize him as Frank Buchanan. He was shooting at the barn.

He looked at the other men and noted that they were also from the town. Confirmation that they were here to save the O'Donnells came when he saw Marshal Granville Coe over by the fence, directing operations. He was launching an attack on the barn. Hudson Gilmore, trapped inside, was now the one who was fighting for his life.

Ryan quickly apprised Alexander of the change in circumstances and with a smile Alexander moved over to the other window to join him in making the situation even tougher for Hudson.

The marshal had recruited at least five deputies and these men had got into positions around the barn, taking advantage of the limited cover afforded by a depression to the left of the house and the fence to the right. As they'd dispatched the two men in the back room, Ryan reckoned that they should now prevail.

With everyone in position the situation quietened for a minute as the marshal waited for Hudson to make his move. When it came, it was a committed one.

Hudson ran out of the barn, brandishing his six-shooter, his men on either side. They'd already picked their targets and while moving quickly they fired to either side in a sustained burst of gunfire that took down two deputies in the initial onslaught. But the rest of the deputies kept their nerve and gunfire exploded from all directions.

One man, then a second went spinning to the ground. A third man, who was already wounded, ran for his horse, but he'd covered only four paces when twin shots to the back sent him to the dirt.

This left just Hudson Gilmore standing, but not for long, as a low shot made blood spray from a leg wound and a second shot to the belly sent him to his knees. He stared down at the ground, seemingly defeated, but then with a great roar of defiance he jerked his gun up and picked out the marshal by the fence.

The two men stared at each other down the barrels of their guns. They both fired.

Hudson fell backwards, his hat flying away and his back becoming arched. He swayed until he rolled over on to his side to display the large hole that marred his forehead.

The attackers dealt with, Ryan strained his neck to

look towards the fence. He winced on seeing two deputies hurrying to the marshal, who was lying on his back, blood spreading on his vest front.

Elsewhere the other deputies came out of hiding to check on the fallen outlaws, so, judging that the situation was under control Ryan headed to the door. He beckoned for Alexander to follow, but with a shake of the head Alexander knelt down beside their dead father, then bade Ryan to move on without him.

Ryan still had too many conflicting emotions about the circumstances leading up to his father's death to join him. Instead he went outside to explain the situation. Frank Buchanan and another deputy, Milton Aldiss, saw him emerging and they both swung their guns round towards him. Ryan holstered his gun, then raised his hands.

'Obliged you came in time,' he said.

Frank licked his lips while eyeing him with delight.

'We heard the shooting,' he said, 'but who would have expected we'd end up here?'

Before Frank could gloat any more Ryan turned his back on him and joined Milton.

'Casey O'Donnell's inside,' he said. 'He's dead.'

Milton nodded, then shepherded him away. Frank moved back into his eye-line to sneer before he hurried on to the house.

Milton stood him by the fence where the other two deputies also acted awkwardly, either not looking at him or casting him darting glances that showed they were confused about how they should treat him.

He leaned back against the fence and watched the two men move on to check on the injured marshal along with the wounded deputies. It appeared that all of the outlaws were probably beyond help.

The men were planning how they'd move the injured when from inside the house Frank shouted an angry oath, making Ryan swing round. Through the window he saw Alexander waving an arm and retorting in kind.

Another sharp exchange sounded. Then a gunshot ripped out. Alexander dropped from view.

With a strangulated plea for help on his lips Ryan broke into a run, but before he reached the porch Milton intercepted him and grabbed him around the shoulders, halting him.

Ryan struggled to get free, but his captor held him with a firm grip. A few moments later Frank came out, holstering his gun, his tread heavy and his face ashen.

'Keep that one held securely,' he said using a broken and shocked tone, 'or he'll do what his brother tried to do.'

Ryan looked to the door, but Alexander was showing no sign of coming out.

'What did he try to do?' Ryan asked with a worried gulp.

'He tried to kill me.' Frank spat. 'But he was the one who got shot up instead, just like your father.'

CHAPTER 7

'I hate doing this,' Sheriff Pilgrim said as he directed Ryan into a cell. 'But the best I can do is, I won't lock the cell.'

'Obliged for that,' Ryan murmured, still feeling too shocked for this one small mercy to comfort him.

This morning he'd had everything he could want. Now he'd lost his brother, his father, his job and probably the respect of everyone who knew him. The only remaining thing for him to lose was his liberty, but even that possibility couldn't worry him now. He was just too shocked.

Pilgrim frowned. 'If it helps, I understand why you had to shelter your father, but I don't reckon many others will see it that way.'

Ryan sat on the cot and thoughtfully rubbed his arm. A sharp pain cut through his stupor and when he removed his hand it was blood-smeared.

'I must have been hit,' he said.

71

Pilgrim leaned forward to appraise the wound, then nodded.

'I'll get you sent to Doctor Tuttle, but it might be a while before he can fix you up. He has a lot of injured men to deal with.'

This comment again reminded Ryan that two of the men he wouldn't have to work on were his kin. He held his head in his hands.

'What will happen to me?' he murmured.

'You harboured an outlaw. You'll be charged. Then you'll have to face the judge and explain yourself.'

Ryan looked up. 'I probably won't be able to do that satisfactorily, but you deserve a proper explanation. I arrested my father and I was set to bring him to town, but Hudson Gilmore arrived before I could leave. That's the truth.'

Pilgrim narrowed his eyes, suggesting he found it hard to believe this version of events. Ryan couldn't blame him.

He had been guarded in his comments to avoid laying blame on his brother, but his limited knowledge of trials told him that only the complete truth would suffice. If he constructed an alternative version of events, eventually his tale would fall apart and make the situation even worse for him.

Yet, no matter how he looked at it, even the truth would sound damning enough to result in a prison sentence.

'I'd like to believe you,' Pilgrim said, his voice strained. He tipped back his hat to rub his forehead. 'But you were gone from town for a long time. . . .'

Ryan nodded. 'I didn't find him straight away and when I did he claimed he had plenty to tell me about what really happened in Kendall Springs last year.'

'He didn't claim he was innocent, did he?'

'My father wasn't exactly a typical outlaw. He was a bungling, hapless opportunist. It always took some believing that he somehow pulled off such a daring raid.' He looked up at Pilgrim, who had flared his eyes showing that he didn't want to entertain the possibility, so he shrugged. 'But as it turned out, he didn't get the chance to speak much and the little he did say didn't make no sense.'

'Then I hope you can work it out because I reckon it's the only thing that'll help you.'

Ryan said nothing else and Pilgrim left him to brood. He leaned back on his cot and with his wounded arm resting on his chest he forced himself to think through the events at his house.

He could recall no more hints about what his father had wanted to tell him and he doubted he would get hold of any additional information from inside a cell.

His arm was throbbing with an insistent rhythm when Pilgrim returned to stand before his cell. Frank Buchanan was at his shoulder, his expression just as thunderous as it had been after he'd shot Alexander.

'Keep him out of my sight,' Ryan muttered, gesturing with his uninjured arm.

'I can't,' Pilgrim said. 'He's escorting you to the doctor.'

'He sure isn't. He shot up my brother.'

'I was just doing my duty as a deputy marshal,' Frank snapped. 'And now I'll do my duty again.'

Ryan snorted. 'Escorting Sheriff Pilgrim's prisoner isn't your duty.'

'Now that's where you're wrong.' Frank came up to the cell door. 'I'm Pilgrim's new deputy sheriff.'

The bodies were still arriving.

Montgomery Pierce had been sleeping on his bed in the corner of Doctor Tuttle's surgery when the first man had been brought in with a gunshot wound. Tuttle had pronounced him to be beyond his help and a few minutes later he'd provided the same prognosis for another man.

This event had been just the first indication of the mayhem that must have taken place as a steady stream of casualties arrived in the two men's wake. Most of the men were almost dead, and only a few were fit enough for the doctor to help them.

Nobody told Montgomery what had happened and he didn't ask. Tuttle was too busy.

Tuttle dealt with the influx at the other end of the surgery. He directed the people he could help to be taken to beds near to Montgomery while the dying were lined up on the floor on the opposite side of the room.

Montgomery raised himself in his bed as far as he could to watch proceedings, but when Tuttle started working on a man with a belly wound he lay down again. He didn't want to be reminded that he'd probably suffered the same operation.

Even though Tuttle worked quickly, before long the groaning from the other wounded men grew in volume.

Montgomery leaned on an elbow to look along the line of beds. Three men were waiting for treatment. They had been arranged in order of priority with the man furthest away from him having heavily packed and bloody bandages wrapped around his right thigh. The man nearest to him had only a cut on the upper arm.

Montgomery flinched when the man looked his way and he saw that it was Deputy Ryan O'Donnell.

'How's my fellow deputy?' Montgomery asked, offering a smile.

'I'm not a deputy no more,' Ryan said, his voice gruff.

'I guess that makes two of us.'

Ryan mustered a smile. 'Except you can be proud of your short term while mine ended in disaster.'

Montgomery asked him to explain what had happened, and since it was clear that he'd have to wait for a while to be treated Ryan detailed the events of

75

the last few hours.

At first he spoke using a faltering voice interspersed with long silences, showing that he didn't want to talk about the incident. But Montgomery encouraged him, and gradually he became more assured as he related his problems.

Unfortunately his confessional only went to make Montgomery feel uneasy, as it started to sound increasingly likely that his guess about what Marshal Coe had whispered to Hudson Gilmore had been right. The marshal really had saved his life by telling him that he needed to find Casey O'Donnell in Prospect Creek.

Montgomery had come to this conclusion after Ryan had left the surgery, but he had made no effort to stay awake for long enough to get that information to him. Now Casey was dead along with Ryan's brother.

Although Montgomery had no way of knowing if the information would have helped to stave off the gunfight, that didn't assuage his sense of guilt.

'I'm sorry,' he said when Ryan had finished his story.

'It's not your fault,' Ryan said. 'You followed the marshal's orders and you weren't involved in the shoot-out, but either way you and he did your duty. I didn't.'

Montgomery frowned. He hadn't meant his comment to be taken that way. It had been a prelude to his revealing the additional information he had, but Ryan was so depressed he decided to keep quiet about his role for now.

'At least the situation's over.'

'Not for me it isn't. My father had a story to tell, but he died before he could tell me all the details.' Ryan fingered around the cut on his arm. 'Perhaps one day I might be able to figure the rest out.'

'Talk to Marshal Coe. He might know how all this fits together.'

Ryan shook his head. 'It's my turn to say that I'm sorry. The marshal won't be able to tell me anything. He was one of the men they brought in.'

Montgomery flopped down on to his bed to look to the ceiling. He hadn't noticed that.

He'd been with the marshal for only a few days and that time had ended with the deaths of three friends, but the marshal had been a decent man and he'd saved his life. Now, like Ryan, he'd probably never find out what the marshal's intentions had been.

'Any of the outlaws survive?'

'I doubt it, but if Tuttle does his usual good work, the marshal will be the only lawman to die.'

Montgomery nodded, finding some comfort in this. He raised himself to look at the men lying opposite, then forced himself up to a sitting position so he could see their faces.

Hudson Gilmore was lying furthest from him, his

form being the bloodiest. In Kendall Springs he had cold-bloodedly killed his friends and he had tried to kill him, but Montgomery felt no elation at seeing him dying.

He looked along the row of men, recognizing most of them from their earlier brief gun battle.

'It's good that Doctor Tuttle kept the marshal apart from these worthless men.'

'I wish he had.' Ryan scowled down the room at a surly looking man who was standing guard by the door. 'Perhaps Deputy Frank Buchanan can do something useful for once and move him to a more dignified place.'

Montgomery looked again at the outlaws, then shrugged.

'The marshal's not here.'

'He is.' Ryan pointed at the man who was lying nearest to them. 'I'm surprised you don't recognize him. You said you rode with him for several days.'

'I did.' Montgomery considered the indicated man, noting that he was one of the few he didn't recognize. 'And I know one thing for sure: that man's not Marshal Coe.'

CHAPTER 8

'Two years for harbouring an outlaw!' Frank said. 'I'd have given you life.'

'Go away,' Ryan said, settling back down on his cot.

Frank laughed, clearly pleased to have goaded him into a response.

'But then again two years in jail for a lawman might as well be life.' Frank tapped his chin, as if he'd just thought of something. 'Before you get locked away, I'll make sure word gets out that you were a deputy sheriff.'

'You'd better make that an effective word, because if I survive I'll be coming back to Prospect Creek and I won't have forgotten what you did to Alexander.'

'Hold on to that anger. It might keep you alive.' Frank laughed. 'But I doubt it.'

He turned away, smiling, and headed back to the desk he'd occupied for the last month after taking over the duties that had been Ryan's.

Previously Ryan had judged Frank to be a wastrel, so in other circumstances his diligence during that month would have impressed him. He had treated the other prisoners who'd come and gone efficiently and fairly, but he could never let pass any opportunity to gloat about Ryan's situation.

As for himself, Ryan had received few visitors and even his former boss had been reluctant to talk to him.

After some consideration, he'd decided not to tell Pilgrim about Montgomery Pierce's concern. And he was glad he hadn't, as at his trial people who knew the marshal had spoken highly of his past activities, proving he had to be the man he said he was.

That meant either Montgomery was lying or the man who had hired him was an impostor. That latter possibility had become more likely when it came to light that the marshal had recently lost his badge.

Even so, neither answer would have helped him, especially as it became clear that as Hudson Gilmore and all of his men had died at the gunfight, he was the only one left to face the justice process. In the cold environment of the court his actions had sounded bad and the townsfolk who had crowded the courtroom had become increasingly hostile.

Nobody had viewed Frank's actions as being anything other than his carrying out his duties as a deputy lawman; in the end he'd been as surprised as Frank was that he'd been handed down only two years.

He'd already resolved that he would serve that time without complaint and afterwards he would try to get answers to the questions his father's story had raised. But he also feared that he wouldn't uncover those answers as his month of pondering about recent events had given him no new insights.

He was to be taken to Sumner Point jail at sunup tomorrow; in view of which he spent a restless last night in the town that had always been his home and which now didn't want him.

His only moment of pleasure came in the morning when Pilgrim relieved Frank, as he would have hated the new deputy to be present for his last moments in town. Although, as always when the sheriff was about, Frank behaved dutifully and he didn't make any unnecessary snide comments.

Pilgrim came up to the bars. 'I've hired someone to take you to jail. He'll be here soon. Don't do anything stupid.'

'I won't.'

The two men looked at each other before Pilgrim began to walk slowly up and down, looking as if he wanted to say something else.

'Before you go,' he said when he stopped pacing, 'you should know that I reconsidered the payroll raid as objectively as I could. It didn't leave me with any obvious loose ends that I can investigate later, so you need to stop worrying about this.'

Ryan considered Pilgrim's guarded comment,

searching for the matter that was clearly worrying him.

'But you have tied up some ends that had previously been loose?'

Pilgrim laughed, showing he'd deduced his concern, but then he bit his lip, seemingly debating whether to continue.

'When I went through your father's possessions I found details of the other three raiders who were thought to have helped him. Previously nobody had known their names for sure, but now I accept they were Leonard Sugg, Hamlin Jenney and Sylvester Howie.'

Ryan had been about to shake his head, but the last name helped him to remember who these people were.

'The three gunslingers who tried to shoot up Edmond Shaffer last month?'

'Yeah. You killed the first two and I hunted Sylvester down. All three men are in the cemetery out of town, but it didn't do Edmond much good in the end. From what Marshal Coe said, he didn't expect to see him alive again.'

'Did the marshal help with the original search for the raiders?' Ryan waited until Pilgrim shook his head. 'Or any other US marshal?'

'Nope. Sheriff Harris spared us that.' Pilgrim sighed. 'As far as I can make out, everyone who was involved with the raid, either rumoured or proven, is now dead.'

'So in the end,' Ryan said, speaking his musings aloud, 'the only remaining loose thread is the missing money. And if everyone who was thought to be connected with its being stolen is now dead, the man who really got away with it is someone whose involvement has never been considered.'

Pilgrim nodded, his glazed eyes suggesting he was pondering. He opened his mouth to reply, but then the door creaked and he turned away to deal with the man who would escort him to jail.

Pilgrim sat on the edge of his desk and outlined his temporary deputy's duties, the likely problems, and the payment.

The deputy would receive twenty dollars now to take Ryan on the two-day journey to the train station at Sunflower City. From there they would embark on an overnight train journey to Sumner Point after which he would be paid another twenty dollars at the jail's door.

'And so,' Pilgrim said finishing off his speech on a positive note, 'I know you can get this job done without mishap. A man who was once a deputy US marshal should be able to deal with a man who was once a deputy sheriff.'

'I reckon so,' Montgomery Pierce said before he turned to the cells to take control of his charge.

'Are you fit again?' Ryan asked when they were five

miles out of town.

'My chest's still sore,' Montgomery said, 'but I'm alive and that's more than I could have expected a month ago.'

They rode on in silence for a while before Ryan turned to Montgomery.

'I've not got the right no more to question a deputy's actions, but are you sure this is the quickest route to Sunflower City?'

Montgomery turned in the saddle and winked.

'It's not. But then again we're not going to Sunflower City.'

Ryan sighed. He had wondered whether Montgomery had an ulterior motive in accepting this mission.

'Obliged for the sentiment,' he said, 'but I've decided I'll accept my punishment. Two years is a fair sentence for my family harbouring an outlaw and I don't intend to start a family tradition by running from justice.'

'I have no intention of helping you escape. I have to get you on the next westward-bound train to leave Sunflower City, and I will. But that still gives us time to get those answers we both need.'

Ryan considered. Despite Montgomery's generous offer, most of those two days would be taken up with travelling, leaving little time to investigate, but Ryan didn't feel inclined to argue.

'Where are we going to first?'

Montgomery gave him a long look. 'Kendall Springs, the place where the payroll was stolen and where the other Marshal Coe went in search of answers of his own.'

'What do you hope to find there?'

'Another dead man whose story has yet to be told.' Montgomery raised a hand when Ryan started to ask for details. 'Only when we get there.'

Then Montgomery diverted the conversation on to talking through the events they had both experienced. As it turned out, Montgomery's ready openness while he shared his version of the situation helped Ryan to accept that he had no reason to lie about Marshal Coe and that he should trust him.

'I don't blame you for not piecing together sooner what the bogus marshal said to Hudson,' Ryan said when they'd finished. He offered a smile that Montgomery returned. 'And even if you had, I wouldn't have acted differently. But it does make me even more determined to find this man who claimed he was a lawman.'

'Me too,' Montgomery said, sounding relieved after Ryan had passed up the opportunity to blame him. 'My friends got shot up on his mission.'

'Why did you join him?'

'The three of us had ridden together on drives for years. We needed the work and also Coe's mission sounded like something that'd give us a tale to tell around the chuck wagon at night, but I'm the only one who survived to tell it.'

'I understand. But what if we can't find any answers in the next two days?'

'Then hopefully I'll have the answers when you get out of jail.'

Ryan nodded and, there being nothing else to discuss, the two men speeded up.

They reached Kendall Springs in late morning. It presented an even more pitiful sight than Ryan had been led to expect. The town had been abandoned after the payroll raid, the newly arrived railroad encouraging many townsfolk to move to Sunflower City and the rest to settle in Prospect Creek.

Then it'd been left to rot. But the fire Hudson had lit reduced what had remained to a sprawling mass of burnt wood that was so low-lying they rode past the town the first time without seeing it.

On returning they rode in along the direction Montgomery had taken when he'd visited the previous month. He stopped on the edge of town to orient himself, then pointed at a ruined building. Burnt wood surrounded a circular patch of flooring that had been largely untouched by flame.

When Montgomery had stared at the patch for a minute Ryan turned to him.

'Was that,' he said, 'where you were found?'

'Yeah,' Montgomery said with a gulp. 'If it's true that the Marshal Coe I met was an impostor and that I was found by the real one, I was lucky not to get burnt alive before the gunshot wound killed me.'

Ryan nodded, then dismounted to go into the ruined saloon while Montgomery hung back. From the road Montgomery pointed out where he'd been shot, the shelter he had crawled into to escape the gunfire, and where the marshal had been strung up.

'You sure did have a lucky escape,' Ryan said, 'but what did you come here to see?'

Montgomery walked to the side of the saloon where the fire had been at its most intense, reducing the wood to ash.

'It'll be over here, but this isn't looking promising.' He waited until Ryan joined him, to stand over the ashes. 'When I hid I came across a body. I reckon it was Edmond Shaffer's, but I don't know why he was here.'

Ryan hunkered down and rooted through the ashes. Anything seemingly substantial disintegrated when he touched it. He looked at Montgomery, shaking his head.

Montgomery stood back to survey the scene. He walked to a spot where several lengths of wood had survived the inferno and moved them aside. Beneath lay blackened bones.

They cleared the area, exposing the full skeleton and making it clear that learning anything about this man, his intentions, and his demise would be impossible. The bones were all that had survived and when Ryan touched a rib the bone crumbled away to dust.

'Did you get a good look at him before he got burnt up?' Ryan said.

'No. I was too busy fighting for my life.' Montgomery looked aloft as he thought back. 'But I remember he was balding with a bushy moustache.'

'That describes the man I met briefly last month.' Ryan sighed, accepting that unfortunately this discovery probably explained his father's statement that before coming to his house he'd done something he wasn't proud of. 'And I reckon Casey O'Donnell waylaid him and killed him before he moved on to Prospect Creek.'

'Except he didn't know he had Hudson Gilmore, Marshal Coe and our mystery man on his tail.' Montgomery considered Ryan's sombre expression. 'But don't think ill of him. If he hadn't killed Edmond, I'd be dead. And we still don't know why he killed him.'

Ryan frowned, unwilling to let this thought lessen his irritation. His father's avoidance of killing anyone while committing his crimes had been the only thing that had given him a small amount of pride, but now even that had gone.

'We're unlikely to answer that or find out anything else about him unless we find Edmond's belongings.'

Montgomery rocked his head from side to side, pondering.

'Which is unlikely. I saw nothing else left lying around.'

Ryan stood and the movement made something glint amongst the ash. When he knelt the object turned out to be a watch. He picked it up and passed it to Montgomery, who turned it over, confirming that the intense heat had melted most of the metal rendering it unusable.

His handling of it made the back fall off, revealing an inscription. He peered at the writing, then shrugged and gave the watch back to Ryan. He struggled to read the ornate letters, which had so many flourishes they would have been hard to read even before the watch had been charred.

'An S and then an H,' he said slowly, then nodded when that assessment sounded right. He passed the watch back to Montgomery.

'I agree, but I don't know anyone with those initials.'

Ryan hadn't considered that the man might be known to him, but he still cast his mind back. He winced.

'But I do,' he said, his thoughts whirling with the possibilities. 'Last month I also briefly encountered a man called Sylvester Howie.'

CHAPTER 9

'Who was Sylvester Howie?' Montgomery asked after he'd placed the last rock over the remains of Edmond Shaffer.

They had found no clues that would explain why Casey had killed him and neither had they found anything else of interest in town, leaving them with no option but to bury the remains before they left.

'He's the reason I became a deputy sheriff,' Ryan said. He went on to describe last month's gunfight.

'Why would Edmond have his watch?' Montgomery asked when he'd finished.

'I don't know. . . .' Ryan narrowed his eyes as a minor recollection of that confrontation came back to him. 'Edmond was told that his time was up and then he felt his pocket. Perhaps Sylvester sent him that watch as a warning that they were coming for him.'

'The only reason I can think of for so many people

to be interested in Edmond is that he knew more about the missing payroll than he ever let on. If we can work out what he knew and find the money, maybe you can be a deputy again.'

Ryan shook his head, but Montgomery then smiled, showing he was trying to sound optimistic to cheer him up. Ryan nodded and they headed back into town.

At the saloon the two men cast their final glances around the derelict town, confirming they were unlikely to learn anything more here. Then they moved for their horses, but they'd taken only a few steps when splinters and ash exploded from a pile of burnt wood before them. The crack of a gunshot sounded a moment later.

The assault was so unexpected the two men stood still for several seconds. Then a second gunshot kicked dirt five feet to the side of them while a simultaneous shot cannoned into the ground to their left as the shooters got them in their sights.

This provided them with all the motivation they needed and, doubled over, they hurried over to the heaped wood and threw themselves to the ground behind it.

'See anyone?' Ryan asked.

For several seconds Montgomery didn't respond; then, moving gingerly, he rolled on to his side and fingered his now mended ribs.

'Nope,' he said with a sigh of relief when he failed

to locate any damage. He patted the top of the wood. 'And there's not many places to hide here.'

'The shots were wild and I haven't seen no horses, so the shooters must be hiding some way away.'

'In that case I can shoot just as wildly as they can.'

Montgomery drew his six-shooter and rested it on the top of the wood. He fired off two quick shots blind. Then he counted to ten and repeated the action before raising himself.

Ryan also raised his head, but he could see nothing untoward.

'Cover me,' he said. 'I'll see if I can get closer to them.'

'All right.' Montgomery winked. 'But just make sure you don't try to escape. I do have cuffs.'

While Ryan smiled, Montgomery reloaded, then placed his gun on the top of the pile. On the count of three Ryan jumped to his feet.

At a run and with his head down Ryan headed for the other side of the road, but no gunfire sounded other than Montgomery's steady shooting and, without mishap, he reached the front of a collapsed building.

He took stock of the situation. Then, moving quickly he worked his way down the road towards the shooters.

He stopped at each building to kneel and look out for them, but he saw no movement and other than the first volley of lead, they hadn't showed themselves again.

After another two hurried dashes forward the growing feeling that he could be walking into a trap overcame him. So when he was facing the hulking shell of the stables, the most intact building in town and so the most likely place for them to be hiding, he stopped and waited.

Long moments passed in silence. When he glanced back down the road Montgomery waved, then briefly raised himself to shrug. With his gaze set on the stables Ryan moved up to a crouching position, then stood with his knees bent.

He was just moving to stand upright when a single shot roared. Ryan dived for cover, leaping over the short wall beside him to lie flat.

In retaliation Montgomery loosed off a wild slug, but when Ryan thought back their assailant's gunshot had been so poorly directed he wasn't even sure where it had landed.

So, heartened, Ryan crawled to the wall and risked peering over it. There was still nobody moving in the stables, but then from the corner of his eye he saw movement. It was some distance out of town.

He caught Montgomery's attention and pointed. Montgomery followed his example and raised himself to a crouched position.

Three riders were emerging from a depression 400 yards out of town. One of the men fired over his shoulder without looking, then they trotted away from town at an unconcerned pace that suggested they weren't worried about being pursued.

Ryan stood to watch them leave, but the men didn't look back, leaving Ryan to pace into the middle of the road and wait for Montgomery to join him.

'Why did they bother?' Ryan asked.

'To let us know they'd seen us,' Montgomery said.

'In which case we now know one thing for sure: there are still people left alive who know something about the missing money.'

Montgomery nodded. Cheered by this thought they returned to their horses.

By the time they'd mounted up and were ready to leave the riders were dots in the distance, but one thing was definite: they were heading towards Sunflower City.

'No luck?' Ryan said when Montgomery returned to their table.

Montgomery shook his head and turned to the door, ready to try the next saloon along the main drag.

Although they'd ridden at a brisk rate they'd still only managed to reach Sunflower City in the early afternoon of the second day of their journey, giving them just a few hours before the train was due. They hadn't encountered the shooters again.

Ryan had kept his spirits up right until the moment when they'd headed to the saloon where

Montgomery had originally been hired as a deputy marshal. They'd learnt nothing. The bartender and several customers had remembered the incident, but they didn't view it as being sinister and they couldn't provide any additional information concerning the marshal.

The next saloon had been just as unhelpful and, as they progressed they got the same story from the other saloons, mercantiles, stables, and lastly the people they stopped in the road as they went about their business.

'I guess,' Montgomery said as their travels brought them closer to the station where people were now congregating, 'it's time for you to make your final decision.'

'I already have,' Ryan said with a heavy sigh. 'I'm getting on that train.'

Montgomery looked up and down the main drag, but they'd tried all the obvious places, so he gestured ahead to the train station.

'Then I won't try to persuade you not to.'

'You shouldn't. If you're going to find anything out, you can't be running from the law too.'

Montgomery nodded, but he didn't look pleased about the prospect of searching alone. In a downbeat manner they headed to the station to join the people gathering on the platform. As it turned out the train was fifteen minutes late in drawing into the station, by which time both men had become resigned to undertaking an unwelcome journey with a sombre ending.

When the train had stopped they dallied while it took on water. So they were the only passengers left waiting to embark when a man ran on to the platform and picked them out.

'You were asking about a marshal recruiting deputies last month?' he said between gasps as he caught his breath.

'Yeah?' Ryan and Montgomery said together.

'Well, there's a man doing something similar right now.' The man pointed to a saloon in an area they'd visited when they'd first arrived. 'Except he never said he was a marshal.'

'What name did he give?' Montgomery asked.

The man rocked his head from side to side as he considered.

'I didn't hear, but he's tall and fair-haired.'

'Obliged,' Montgomery said with a nod at Ryan, indicating that he knew the man's identity. He rooted in his pocket, then dropped a few coins in the man's hand. In his distracted state he didn't even look at how much he paid him before he turned to Ryan. 'What are we doing about this?'

As the man walked away, content with his payment, Ryan looked to the indicated saloon, then to the train. The engineer was looking out of the engine and the doors were being checked in preparation of moving out.

'I'm not failing to turn up at the jail before sundown tomorrow,' he said. He considered the flash of disappointment in Montgomery's eyes. 'But then again I don't have to get on that train.'

Montgomery slapped his shoulder. 'This is the best chance we'll ever get to find out who our mystery man is. So once we've done that, we'll do some hard riding and board the train at the next station.'

With that agreement the men hurried after their informer, catching up with him fifty yards from the saloon. By this time the train was lurching into motion, but Ryan felt only elation at the prospect of making real progress before his liberty was curtailed.

They stopped at the saloon door to consider a scene that was similar to the one when the real Marshal Granville Coe had ridden into Prospect Creek seeking help. A man at the bar was talking loudly while most of the customers avoided meeting his eye.

'Him?' Ryan asked.

Montgomery gave a brief nod. Then he put on a wide smile and looked at Ryan until he also mustered a false smile. With Montgomery leading, they entered the saloon slowly, letting the marshal spot them before they reached the bar.

Ryan was pleased to see that Granville twitched with surprise and perhaps a little concern before he noticed Montgomery's smile and got his feelings under control.

97

'Is that you, Montgomery?' he asked cautiously.

'It sure is, Marshal Granville Coe,' Montgomery said, in a loud and boisterous tone that ensured everyone heard his name. 'Thanks to you.'

Granville winced before he beckoned him on. Several of the men who had been listening to him frowned and glanced at each other, suggesting they'd been given a different name. And the speed with which they then sidled off suggested he hadn't been pretending to be a lawman either.

'I wasn't sure you'd live,' Granville said.

'Neither was I. I lay unconscious for hours, but when I came to Doctor Tuttle told me you'd got me to Prospect Creek.'

Even though he knew the truth Ryan couldn't detect the subterfuge in Montgomery's light tone. When Granville had considered his statement he nodded, although he couldn't suppress a relieved sigh.

'So what do you want to do now?'

'It looks as if you still want help, so I want to join you.' Montgomery patted his chest. 'I'm mended, I've proved myself, and I'm ready for more.'

Granville nodded then glanced past him at Ryan.

'And who's your friend?'

Ryan moved forward and introduced himself, although he gave a different surname. Then, figuring that Montgomery was being too cautious with his approach he watched for Granville's reaction to his revelation.

98

'I heard that in the end you shot up that loco railroad man Hudson Gilmore, so I figure Montgomery's right about you and that you're a man to support.'

Granville smiled, appearing unconcerned, but, after all, he'd now had enough time to get his surprise under control. The men he'd been addressing before were now ignoring him and Granville looked at them while nodding to himself, as if weighing up whether to take the bait.

'In that case I'm still looking for Edmond Shaffer; that interest you?'

Ryan cast a narrowed-eyed glance at Montgomery, silently asking him not to say that they'd found his body in Kendall Springs.

'It might do,' Montgomery said.

Granville considered them with a smile on his lips. Then with a determined shrug of his jacket he patted both men on the back and slipped past them.

'Then I'll see you both later,' he called over his shoulder as he headed to the door with unseemly haste, 'when I've seen if anyone else wants to join our search.'

Ryan shuffled closer to Montgomery at the bar and together they watched him leave. Outside Granville walked stiffly in a self-conscious manner and didn't look back.

'He's knows something's wrong,' Ryan said.

'That doesn't matter,' Montgomery said. 'It's not

as if we're joining him. We'll give him a minute then see where he goes.'

Ryan nodded. Through the window they watched Granville walk away. When he reached the end of the road they went to the door, where they waited while Granville stopped and glanced around. Then he turned left to walk away from the station.

The moment he disappeared from view around the corner of a building they hurried outside. They'd managed only two paces when rapid footfalls pattered, approaching from behind. Ryan started to turn, but cold steel jabbed into the back of his neck, halting him.

'Now where are you two going in a hurry?' a harsh voice muttered in his ear.

Ryan glanced to the side. He was surprised to find that Deputy Frank Buchanan had accosted him.

He raised his hands slightly then shook his head at Montgomery telling him not to retaliate. The three men walked towards an alley.

'What are you doing here?' Ryan asked when they were standing in the shadows beside the saloon.

'Sheriff Pilgrim was worried that you wouldn't get on that train,' Frank said. He glanced away to glimpse the train that was now receding into the distance. 'He said if you're not on it, you're an escaped prisoner.'

Montgomery stepped up to Frank's side. 'This man remains my responsibility until I get him to

Sumner Point jail. How I choose to get him there is no concern of yours or Sheriff Pilgrim's.'

'As you've missed the train you should now be riding fast to reach Sumner Point in time,' Frank said, smirking with confidence that he was in the right here. 'Except you two are wasting away the afternoon in a saloon.'

'That's because we were talking with Marshal Granville Coe.'

Frank had already opened his mouth to pour scorn on Montgomery's retort, but when the words registered he shook himself, then manoeuvred Ryan to the side. He removed the gun from his neck, although he didn't holster it as he backed away for a pace so that he could keep both men in view.

'What are you two scheming about?'

'Nothing,' Montgomery said. 'What I said was the truth. Marshal Granville Coe was in the saloon just now looking to recruit a new batch of deputies.'

'So perhaps,' Ryan said, 'as you enjoyed such a successful mission with him the last time you might want to join him again?'

Frank looked to the end of the road, indicating that he had seen Granville leave.

'If that's who that man claimed himself to be,' he said, his tone becoming uncertain, suggesting he was starting to believe their story, 'he's an impostor, and a bad one at that.'

Ryan nodded. 'Frank, despite everything, you may

one day become a good deputy lawman. That's what we figured, except you stepped in before we could find out what his plan is.'

'You're a prisoner. You have no right to do anything but go to jail.' Frank turned to Montgomery. 'And you shouldn't have dealt with this yourself. You should have reported this impostor and then taken your prisoner to jail.'

'I guess that's why you're the deputy sheriff of Prospect Creek,' Montgomery said, making Ryan smile when he adopted this sarcastic attitude. 'I just didn't know what to do for the best.'

Frank looked again to the end of the road, and for the first time Ryan felt a twinge of sympathy for his predicament. If he were to put aside his hatred of him, he could see that Frank took his duties seriously.

Frank nodded, as if he'd made his decision.

'Tell me everything,' he said. 'I'll deal with the impostor. Then I'll make sure Ryan gets to jail where he belongs.'

'There's not much to tell,' Montgomery said, speaking in a matter-of-fact manner. 'The man who claimed to be Marshal Granville Coe is still aiming to track down the missing railroad man Edmond Shaffer.'

Frank glanced away, but not before Ryan saw his eyebrows shoot up. He tipped back his hat while considering; then, to Ryan's surprise, he gestured down the road.

'Then I reckon,' he said, 'we'd better join his band of deputies before he hightails it out of town.'

CHAPTER 10

'So now all three of you want to join me?' Granville said.

'Sure,' Frank said, taking the lead. He sat down, then gestured around the saloon room, taking in the customers, none of whom was looking their way. 'And from the look of it nobody else wants to do the job.'

In reality Ryan doubted that Granville had even mentioned his intentions. When they'd first seen him he'd been heading for the stables, while looking over his shoulder. But when he'd seen that he was being followed he'd ducked into the nearest saloon and taken refuge at a table in a dark corner.

Granville lowered his head in a defeated manner before he spoke.

'Why not, then? I'll swear you all in as deputy marshals.'

'And on that I can help you.' Frank smiled. 'I

know plenty about Edmond Shaffer's movements.'

Earlier Frank had demanded to take the lead in trying to work out what Granville's true intent was, so Ryan and Montgomery didn't react. For his part Granville narrowed his eyes and leaned forward over the table.

'You know a lot for a man who just happened to come into a saloon with these two.'

'I do,' Frank said levelly, leaning back in his chair, 'but if you reckon you have better information, we'll follow that instead. You are, after all, in charge.'

Granville rubbed his jaw as he pondered, but before he could reply shadows spread out over the table. When Ryan turned it was to see that three men had arrived. They were standing a few feet apart covering all the directions they could take to leave the corner of the saloon.

'We heard you're looking for Edmond Shaffer,' one man said.

Granville cast his three seated colleagues an amused smile, then gestured for the newcomers to join them at the table. They didn't move.

'Now Edmond sure is mighty popular,' Granville said. 'Why does he interest you?'

'Because we work for the railroad.'

'I'd heard that some railroad men got shot to pieces recently in Prospect Creek.'

The man's right eye twitched. 'Unlike Hudson Gilmore, we still work for the railroad. We aim to

105

keep things that way and that means avoiding the mistakes Hudson made.'

Granville leaned back, but he said nothing. The men glanced at each other, silently considering their next move. Something about their stances let Ryan place where he'd seen them before.

It'd been from a distance, but their interest in Edmond made him sure. If he didn't have the deadline of reaching jail, he'd have bided his time and let them make the first move. Instead, he leaned forward.

'Except,' he said, 'you three all reckon Edmond was killed in Kendall Springs, so why are you claiming you're looking for him?'

The man cast a sideways glance at his colleagues. Then he threw his hand to his holster.

Unarmed, Ryan did the only thing he could do. He leapt out of his chair and with a frantic gesture he lunged for the table. He upended it and twisted it towards the three newcomers.

Two men avoided the table easily, but it caught the nearest man's gun arm pushing his hand down as he fired. His gunshot blasted into the floor as Ryan threw himself at him.

He was several feet away from his target and the man easily swayed away to avoid his lunge, but then he had other problems to deal with as everyone else around the table went for their guns.

A moment later two gunshots tore into the chest

of Ryan's quarry from Frank's and Granville's guns. While both men each went for one man, Montgomery took on the man in the middle, so Ryan doubled back, aiming to subdue the third man.

His target was swinging his gun towards Granville. If he'd aimed at Ryan instead, Ryan would have been dead before he could reach him, but the extra moments it took for the gunman to turn let Ryan gather momentum and barge into him.

He hit the gunman in the side with a leading shoulder, bundling him over as he fired. The shot slammed high into the wall, but as the man fell he caught Ryan's legs, with his own sprawling legs bringing him down with him.

They both landed on their sides on the floor where Ryan scrambled for his opponent's gun. He slapped his right hand on his wrist and then moved to wrest the gun with his left hand, but the man twisted away forcing Ryan to go tumbling over him.

Gunfire tore out as his companions locked horns, and feet scuffled as the other customers hurried to get out of the way of the fight. Ryan put them from his mind and concentrated on his battle. He rolled over his opponent and the entangling of their limbs ensured they rolled towards the wall.

They struggled, but neither man got the upper hand as they upended several chairs and another table. Two more shots rang out and someone cried out. The cry was closely followed by the thud of a

107

body hitting the floor. Ryan resisted the urge to see who had fallen as he fetched up against the wall.

Trapped with his back to the wall Ryan struggled to free himself as the man pressed up close. With his arms caught between the two of them he couldn't stop the man bringing his gun down, then aiming towards his face.

Another shot sounded. The gun continued to move until it was inches away from Ryan's right eye. Then the gun halted and a spasm made his assailant's back arch. A moment later Ryan realized that the last gunshot had hit the man in the side.

Taking advantage of his weakness, he tore the gun from the man's weakening grip and fought his way to his feet. He stood over his assailant with the gun aimed down at his chest, but the man was now still.

Ryan looked towards the table; it was lying on its side. The second attacker lay sprawled backwards over the edge with his arms dangling and gunsmoke rising from his chest.

The third gunman sat propped up against a leg, his slack arms clutching a bloodied belly. As Ryan watched the man slid sideways and lay on the floor in a heap.

Standing around them were Granville, Frank and Montgomery. None of them appeared to have been harmed.

'Glad you got yourself a gun,' Granville said with a wink. 'I've got no use for an unarmed deputy.'

Ryan nodded while, to his credit, Frank went to one knee and riffled through the pockets of the nearest fallen man. The others joined him in his quest, but their quick search failed to confirm who these men were.

'So you're lawmen,' a man said behind Ryan. Ryan turned to find that five customers had lined up along the bar.

Most of the men were eyeing the door, clearly wishing they were elsewhere, but the bartender had a rifle trained on Granville and two other men had drawn guns. Other seated customers were leaning back with grim expressions on their faces and their hands hidden beneath tables.

'Sure,' Granville said. He stood up and paced to the front. He looked along the row of men, then back until he faced the man who had spoken. 'You got a problem?'

'We haven't. You might.'

Granville glanced down at his gun. Then with a shrug he holstered it slowly, making several men in the line relax. He glanced over his shoulder at the others. One by one they holstered their guns. Ryan tucked his gun in his belt.

'And why might a US marshal have a problem?' Granville took two long steps forward to stand before the speaker.

The man nervously rubbed his chin and looked to his colleagues for support, but the initial truculence had gone from many of them and even the bar-tender had lowered his rifle.

'None, I guess.'

'Good.' Granville turned to the door, but then with a sudden motion he turned on his heel and with a backhanded swipe he slapped the man's cheek, sending him reeling into the bar. He stood over him as the man righted himself. 'Don't ever hold a gun on a lawman again.'

Without further comment he strode to the door with Ryan and the other two trailing in his wake.

'The man had a point,' Frank said when they were outside.

Granville glared at him, but he said nothing. Ryan pointed back at the saloon.

'You do need to explain to someone in authority,' he said, 'that you'd already deputized us before that gunfight.'

Granville kept walking at a brisk pace.

'You can waste time explaining yourselves,' he muttered. 'I've got a man to find.'

Granville strode on towards the stables. In quick order they mounted their horses, after which they left town quickly and before the town marshal could come to question them, giving further credence to the belief that Granville was an impostor who could-n't risk being probed.

Thankfully nobody followed them out of town as they galloped on, heading west. After three miles they slowed and bunched up to talk.

'You got a destination in mind?' Frank asked.

'The railroad office is in Sumner Point,' Granville said. 'I reckon we should go there and find out why those men were so aggrieved.'

Ryan had no complaints about this plan and although Frank cast him a sneering glance Montgomery accepted his order with a relieved smile. They spread out as they hurried on and for the rest of the afternoon they moved on at a mile-eating pace.

As they'd spent more time in town than they'd planned they didn't catch sight of the train. But when the other two riders were riding out of earshot Montgomery reported to Ryan that even if they had to ride all the way, they should still be able to reach the jail before sundown tomorrow.

Only when they had pitched camp for the night and were sitting around a roaring fire did Granville ask the question Ryan had expected since the gun-fight.

'What did you mean about Edmond Shaffer being killed in Kendall Springs?'

Before he answered Ryan glanced at Montgomery, who nodded.

'We came across his body lying amidst the ruined buildings. We reckon Casey O'Donnell killed him, but we can't prove that. Everything Edmond owned had been burnt to ashes except for a watch.'

111

Ryan looked at Montgomery, who withdrew the watch from his pocket and held it up.

'The initials,' he said, 'on the back are SH, which we reckon means it belonged to one of his fellow raiders, Sylvester Howie.'

'Give it to me,' Frank snapped, thrusting out a hand.

Granville twitched, his expression a mixture of surprise and curiosity that he managed to control by leaning forward to poke the fire. As Ryan watched him, wondering what his reaction had meant, Montgomery did as requested. Then Ryan continued with their explanation while Frank examined the watch.

'Then the three railroad men we met in the saloon arrived and tried to shoot us up.'

'Pity they didn't kill you the first time,' Frank muttered, turning the watch over in his hand.

Ryan bristled, but Granville nodded slowly, while looking from one man to the other as he observed their apparent animosity.

'Do you reckon,' Granville said, 'that Edmond stole it?'

Frank clutched the watch tightly before he leaned back and relaxed.

'Perhaps,' he said before Ryan could answer. His voice caught and he coughed to clear his throat suggesting this matter was more important to him than he would wish to show.

112

'Or,' Ryan said, 'Edmond had more to do with the payroll raid than anyone suspects and that's why Sylvester wanted him dead and then later Casey killed him.'

Granville smiled thinly, as if this suggestion was an obvious one that he'd already considered.

'You still reckon,' Frank said, 'we should go to Sumner Point, then?'

Granville nodded. 'If Edmond's dead, that's the only place we'll get answers.'

'You're right,' Frank said, smirking as he regained his former surly mood. 'The two of us might find something out.'

'What about the four of us?'

With Frank grinning but saying nothing, Ryan spoke up.

'He means that I'm a prisoner. Montgomery is taking me to jail and I won't get to leave Sumner Point.'

Granville accepted this information without any noticeable reaction while Frank nodded approvingly, then backed away from the fire to settle down for the night.

He didn't return the watch.

CHAPTER 11

After their debate, the mismatched group didn't speak again that night.

The next morning they set off before first light and continued on their westward route, which turned out to be more direct than the one the train took, making Ryan sure that he'd reach their destination that day.

What would happen on the journey was less certain.

Despite agreeing to let them join him and the bonding that fighting off the railroad men together should have inspired, Granville Coe was a quiet and reluctant leader. He rode as far from the others as possible, presumably in case of duplicity. Ryan got the impression he knew there was something amiss with their joining him, but he wasn't sure what it was.

His distrust was a minor problem compared to the animosity amongst the others.

Ryan couldn't stop himself from shooting aggrieved glares at Frank, while surprisingly Frank reserved most of his glaring for Granville. Montgomery was the most content, but he was pensive, presumably with worry about whether he would be able to complete his task of getting Ryan to jail in time.

With nobody in the mood for dallying they made good time. They reached Sumner Point in late afternoon of what would be Ryan's last day of freedom for a while. Granville led them on a detour around town to come in beside the railroad station. He rode hunched in the saddle with his hat drawn down low.

The other men didn't comment on his furtive behaviour, each being taken up with his own thoughts.

Montgomery would have to escort Ryan to the prison, a large compound beyond the edge of town. The prospect made it hard for him to look Ryan in the eye, while Ryan had become resigned to his fate.

He didn't expect to learn anything now that would stop him brooding about the unsolved mysteries during his sentence, but he still followed dutifully after Granville to a saloon, where Granville dismounted quickly and scurried inside.

From here they could look out at both the railroad station and the jail. Granville took a table near the window, where he nursed a coffee while looking through the window. The other men joined him.

'So,' Ryan said, figuring the others wouldn't speak, 'are you going to ask questions about Edmond and those railroad men?'

'Been here before,' Granville said, his low tone confirming he'd faced trouble of the kind they'd encountered in Sunflower City. 'I'm not asking anyone anything, but I will get answers.'

He leaned back to let them have a better view of the scene outside, then pointed across the road at the large office building beside the station.

'When are we going to the railroad office?' Frank asked. He cast Ryan a smirking glance that said this would be a task Ryan wouldn't be involved in.

Granville winked. 'Shortly, when the office's closed.'

Frank snorted a supportive laugh, but Ryan frowned as the last chance for him to learn anything before his incarceration faded. And he became even more sombre when Granville decided to scout around the office to work out what would be the best way to break in.

Without comment Frank joined him, although he stopped in the doorway to favour Ryan with a cheery and mocking wave. Ryan ignored him, finding solace in the fact that he wouldn't have to suffer his company during his last hour as a free man.

For a while he and Montgomery sat in silence, until Montgomery leaned forward.

'Shall I leave you alone?' he asked.

116

'Do your duty to the last,' Ryan said. He offered a smile. 'And as I don't reckon I could cope with the temptation of being free to run, I'd hate to get a fellow deputy into trouble.'

Montgomery smiled, but he didn't reply as the bartender was coming over to refill their coffees.

'I hadn't realized you were lawmen,' the man said in a conversational manner as he filled their mugs with practised speed, having clearly heard some of their conversation.

'It's not obvious, then?' Montgomery asked.

'No.' He nodded to the window. 'But I guess I was just surprised you were sitting with that other man. I don't know who he is, but he avoided the last lawman to come in here.'

Montgomery and Ryan glanced at each other and nodded as, for the first time, they got a clue about who Granville really was.

'Who was that lawman?' Montgomery said.

The bartender looked up as he thought back.

'Marshal Granville Coe.' The bartender rubbed his chin. 'He was asking about Edmond Shaffer just after he'd been reported missing. I don't know what he learnt, but he left town in a hurry and a bad mood.'

'I'd heard he'd mislaid his badge,' Montgomery said.

The bartender shrugged, then resorted to general time-passing prattle before he headed back to the bar.

'I reckon we've now just about pieced together,' Ryan said when the bartender had gone, 'what our unwelcome colleague was doing before he hired you and how he came to assume the marshal's identity.'

Montgomery nodded. 'And it all points to him being eager to find Edmond so he could find out what he knew about the payroll.'

Ryan sighed, then looked out of the window. He judged that he had thirty minutes of freedom before his sundown deadline and he was almost tempted to spend that time peacefully, but he took a long sip of his coffee and then stood up.

'Come on,' he said. 'We need to stop whatever Granville's planning to do.'

They walked outside calmly and then crossed the road. They confirmed that the railroad office had just closed, then set about roaming around the vicinity, and then around the station and the tracks, searching for Frank and Granville. They couldn't find either man.

When they'd completed a full circle and they were heading back to the saloon their behaviour started to gather odd looks from passers-by. Thankfully, before anyone waylaid them Montgomery pointed down the alley between the office and the next building. There was an open window there that Ryan was sure hadn't been open before.

They went to investigate.

One shutter was open, but nobody was visible in

118

the small room beyond and all was quiet. Ryan turned to Montgomery, meaning to ask him whether they should investigate inside, when Frank stepped out of a doorway further down the alley.

'Get over here,' he urged, 'before anyone sees you.'

Ryan and Montgomery both glanced along the road, but nobody was passing, so they joined him in the doorway.

'Perhaps they should,' Ryan said.

'Granville's activities are no concern of yours. You're a prisoner and soon you'll be locked up where you belong.'

'I'm only thinking of your welfare. If you're going to enjoy a more successful term as Pilgrim's deputy than I did, you don't want to get involved with men like Granville Coe, or whatever his name is.'

Frank had been sneering while Ryan spoke, but when he finished he merely waved at him in a dismissive manner, then looked at Montgomery.

'Take him to jail and stop him annoying me.'

'I intend to,' Montgomery said, 'but we deputies have to help each other out and Ryan's right. You shouldn't ride with a man who's clearly up to no good. He might even have been involved in the original payroll theft.'

'He might have been,' Frank said, shrugging, 'or he might be trying to work out what happened to the money. When I find out the truth, I'll deal with it

119

myself as a lawman.'

'Then do that, but don't risk doing it on your own.'

Frank opened his mouth to snap back a retort, but then with a sigh he lowered his head.

'I have to,' he said using a low tone that was different from his previous belligerent attitude.

'Why?' Ryan asked, also speaking more calmly than before.

Frank leaned forward to look out of the doorway at the window from where rustling, then a cracking of wood sounded, suggesting Granville had found something of interest. He kicked at the dust, then briefly looked Ryan in the eye for one of the rare times.

'Because,' Frank said, as the sounds of destruction coming from within the office grew, 'he might uncover the truth about why Sylvester Howie tried to kidnap Edmond Shaffer.'

'Why does that concern you?' Ryan asked. He waited, but Frank didn't reply. 'Sylvester was one of the men who was thought to be involved in the raid and—'

'And he was my brother,' Frank muttered. Then having uttered the words he softened his tone. 'My half-brother, that is. I'd never known where he was until one day he just rode into town.'

'And five minutes later I drove him off when I stopped his colleagues taking Edmond away.' Ryan considered. 'Is that why you hate me beyond all reason?'

Frank gave a barely perceptible nod. 'You ruined my only chance of meeting him. Can you blame me for hating you?'

Ryan narrowed his eyes. 'Except I didn't kill Sylvester; Sheriff Pilgrim did.'

Frank licked his lips, regaining some of his usual surly demeanour.

'I know, and so now I work for him, biding my time. One day he'll tell me about the time he killed my brother, and then. . . .'

Frank trailed off and performed a mime of a quick knife-slash across the throat. When that information had registered and made Ryan gulp, he moved out into the alley, but Ryan grabbed his shoulder and drew him back.

'I won't let you kill Pilgrim,' he muttered.

'You can't stop me.'

Frank slapped his hand away and moved on purposefully to the window, where scraping sounded a moment before Granville glanced out. He was frowning and when he saw Frank he held out a hand for him to help him clamber out.

'I've found it,' he said when Frank linked hands with him. 'I now know why Casey O'Donnell killed Edmond Shaffer and where the payroll is.'

121

CHAPTER 12

'What have you found out?' Frank said.

Granville jumped down to the ground where he noted Ryan's presence with a brief scowl. He turned to Montgomery.

'I'll tell you about it,' he said, 'once this deputy has left to do his duty.'

'We still have enough time,' Montgomery said, 'to hear what you found in there.'

Granville shrugged, then withdrew a folded sheet of paper from his pocket. He gestured with it at Ryan, then slipped it away.

'Only those who are leaving town with me need to know.'

Frank nodded and swung round to face Montgomery and Ryan.

'You heard him,' he said. 'We're leaving. You're going to jail.'

Granville moved to set off down the alley and

Frank turned to leave with him, but Ryan hurried to them and raised his arms, blocking their way.

'Neither of you is going nowhere until you tell me what you learnt in there.'

Granville cast him a disdainful glare. 'You don't give the orders here.'

'Maybe not, but if I tell the guards at the jail that you broke into the railroad office, I reckon it'll get me a shorter sentence.'

Frank sneered, but the threat made Granville step up to Ryan.

'I can make things even harder for you in there,' he muttered. 'Don't say nothing.'

Ryan smiled. 'That threat tells me everything I need to know about you. You're trying to get your hands on the payroll money.'

Granville grunted with anger. With a firm hand he shoved Ryan away, sending him reeling into the wall. By the time Ryan had righted himself Granville was striding purposefully towards the entrance to the alley and Montgomery was hurrying after him.

Ryan glanced at Frank, who shook his head and moved to follow Granville. He'd managed two paces when Ryan lunged. He wrapped an arm around his shoulders from behind and drew him to a halt.

Frank perhaps hadn't expected Ryan to accost him, as for several seconds he didn't fight back. Instead he watched Montgomery catch up with Granville, then start remonstrating with him. When

Granville brushed Montgomery aside, Frank braced himself with a satisfied grunt then tried to throw Ryan aside, but Ryan had a firm hold and he stood his ground.

'Let go of me, prisoner,' Frank muttered.

Ryan noted the red light of the lowering sun playing on the buildings beyond the entrance to the alley.

'I'm not a prisoner yet,' he muttered, 'but if you follow him, you will be soon.'

'That's my choice.'

'It is, but after all the scorn you poured on me for being the son of an outlaw, I find it interesting that you're the brother of one and that your main aim in life is to kill a lawman.'

'Sure is,' Frank said with a roll of his shoulders that failed to dislodge Ryan's grip. 'And there's nothing you can do to stop me.'

'I don't need to. Pilgrim will take care of a nobody like you without breaking sweat.'

Frank grunted with anger, then dropped to one knee. His unexpected movement surprised Ryan and as he had a firm grip around Frank's shoulders he was lifted bodily off the ground.

Unable to keep his balance he rolled forward, then went tumbling over Frank's shoulders to land on his back. He shook himself and moved to get up, but then he had to jerk aside to avoid Frank's boot as he tried to stamp on him.

With his back to his assailant he couldn't avoid a swiping kick to the rump, but that didn't stop him gaining his feet, where he settled his balance and turned with his fists raised.

Frank appraised him with a sneering expression. Then he also raised his fists and turned to stand side-on to him.

With his opponent accepting they would sort out their differences now, Ryan took his time. Slowly he walked in a circle around Frank, who followed him by turning on the spot.

His steady progress let Ryan see down the alley. At the other end Montgomery was faring badly. Granville had bested him and was holding him pressed up against the wall. An angry muttered conversation was in progress in which clearly Montgomery was trying and failing to get answers.

With a shake of the head Ryan tore his gaze away from the altercation, but he acted too slowly and Frank was already taking advantage of his distracted state.

A swiping blow came swinging round at his head and Ryan couldn't avoid it. The fist pummelled his cheek and sent him reeling. Frank followed him and then the blows came quickly and strongly.

Another swinging blow slugged his cheek in the opposite direction, knocking him backwards into the wall. Then an uppercut to the point of the chin stood him upright; it was closely followed by a short-armed jab to the stomach that blasted all the air from his chest and made him double over.

He staggered forward for a pace, seeking refuge from his resolute opponent, but Frank stepped to the side. With doubled fists he clubbed the back of his neck, sending him to his knees.

Ryan swayed, then toppled over on to his side. He lay gasping and trying to regain his strength, but the moment he looked up it was to face Frank's swinging boot, which thudded into his cheek and rolled him on to his back.

As his vision swirled a second kick caught him a glancing blow behind the ear. The blow must have made him black out as the next thing he was aware of was someone groaning. The thought came only slowly that he was the one making the noise. Then he grunted in pain when Frank contemptuously walked over him and ground a foot into his stomach.

Frank made his way to the wall where he turned and leaned back. He looked down at Ryan with contempt in his eyes as he slowly gathered his senses.

'And you claim to be a son of Casey O'Donnell,' Frank said. 'You and Alexander were never good enough to say that.'

This was such an odd taunt to make that Ryan forced himself to move. He pushed himself back along the ground then rolled. He put a hand out to the wall to steady himself before he forced himself up to a sitting position.

He doubted he had the energy to fight back just yet, so he contented himself with glaring up at Frank and committing his form to memory for his stay in jail.

'Our father never did nothing we were proud of, so we were ashamed to be known as his sons.'

'I know,' Frank snapped, pushing himself from the wall to loom over Ryan. 'And if I was minded, I'd kill you for that too. But I reckon I'll let prison knock the arrogance out of you first.'

Frank opened and closed his fists as if he were still minded to pummel him some more, but then with a jerking movement he swung away and headed down the alley.

'You know I'll be coming for you,' Ryan shouted after him.

Frank took two more paces then stopped. He snorted a laugh, but he didn't turn, so Ryan pushed himself to his knees. He still felt too weak from his pummelling to gain his feet and contented himself with glaring at his back.

At the end of the alley Montgomery was lying propped up against the wall, unmoving and appearing as defeated in his attempt to take on his nemesis, as Ryan was. Granville had gone.

'I know,' Frank said in a quiet voice. He turned and looked him over as if he too were committing his form to memory in preparation of the later conclusion to their feud. 'And then out of the four, there'll be one.'

Frank gave a slight smile, suggesting he wanted Ryan to ask him what his cryptic comment had meant.

'Four?' Ryan asked, making Frank's smile broaden.

'The sons of Casey O'Donnell.'

Ryan's already battered guts lurched and he stared at Frank agog.

'What you trying to tell me?'

'That Casey O'Donnell was wayward in all ways. You and Alexander weren't the only sons he sired. He lived over this way for a while. Sylvester Howie was the result.'

Ryan closed his eyes as he pieced together the situation.

'Casey told me he'd lost a son over that payroll raid, but I didn't realize he was talking about his son Sylvester.' He gulped as the other aspect of this revelation hit him. 'And Sylvester was your half-brother.'

He opened his eyes to see that Frank was heading off down the alley.

'He was,' Frank said, not looking back, 'and so I lost a father and a brother. That means the money's rightfully mine.'

Frank stopped beside Montgomery. He looked down at his slumped form, shook his head, then headed out into the road.

'More importantly,' Ryan shouted after him, 'it means we're both sons of Casey O'Donnell.'

Frank didn't look back and a few moments later he disappeared from view around the corner.

His shock giving him renewed energy, Ryan crawled along the alley. He went past the groaning Montgomery, then looked out along the road. Frank and Granville weren't visible, so he turned back to Montgomery.

'It's not looking good,' Montgomery murmured. He patted his ribs gently and winced. 'I reckon that beating's reopened my old wound.'

'Then sit and rest awhile.' Ryan shuffled round to sit beside him. The light was dim now. 'Did you hear what Frank said?'

'Yeah, and that means we have enough information now to piece this all together.'

'You might have. I've got about five more minutes of freedom and then I'm an escaped prisoner.'

'And I'm a failed deputy.'

Montgomery looked at him with his eyebrows raised, silently asking him the obvious question; this time Ryan gave it serious consideration before he shook his head.

'For me, answers will have to wait.'

'I thought you'd say that.' Montgomery slipped his hand into his jacket. His fumblings made him wince, but when he found what he was looking for he mustered a smile. Then he withdrew a folded sheet of paper. 'You need to read this first before you make such statements.'

'What is it?'

'Granville wouldn't answer my questions, so while he was busy giving me a beating I concentrated on getting this off him. It's the letter he stole from the railroad office.'

With a glance at the fading light playing on the buildings out on the road Ryan took the paper and opened it up.

The document turned out to be a copy of a letter written by Edmond Shaffer and dated one year earlier. It confirmed the details of the payroll's route, giving places and times. Those details were classed as secret.

Ryan read it through, but he saw nothing else of interest.

'This might prove Edmond was involved in helping others to rob his own railroad, but I can't see why it excited Granville so much.'

'Read it again, carefully. It gave Granville all the answers he needed.'

Ryan did as asked, this time running his gaze over the entire letter. Then with a gulp he noticed whom the letter had been sent to. He looked aloft.

'And it answers mine too,' he murmured.

CHAPTER 13

'You only just got here on time,' Doctor Willis said, 'and I've not got the time to waste on malingerers.'

Montgomery took tentative steps across the surgery, then leaned his weight on the doctor's table. He didn't have to exaggerate the pain he was in as every movement sent bolts of fire knifing through his chest. He must have conveyed his predicament, as without further complaint Willis bade him to lie down on the table.

He didn't help him, so Montgomery swung himself gingerly on to the table. With a hand clutched to his stomach he tried to lie flat, but stretching proved to be too painful, so he lay on his side curled up.

Willis considered him with a sceptical eye, then gestured at him to remove the hand. Montgomery moved it slowly, but doing so helped him to relax and when Willis laid hands on his chest some distance

131

from the centre of the pain he unwound himself and by degrees he stretched until he was lying flat.

'I got shot and stitched up a month ago,' he said.

'And then today you got into. . . .' Willis trailed off when his probing made Montgomery bleat and double over. He straightened him out before continuing, 'you got into more trouble?'

'Yeah, a few hours ago.'

'Your behaviour doesn't bode well for your future.'

Montgomery took deep breaths, but when he didn't reply immediately Willis raised his vest and considered the mottled skin with his jaw set firm.

'What about my immediate future?' Montgomery whispered.

'You'll be fine. Your original wound will have healed by now. You won't have ruined your previous doctor's good work.'

'Then why does it hurt so much?'

Willis poked with a firm finger, provoking a sharp intake of breath.

'This time you probably have a cracked rib. I'll bind your chest and then you need to avoid taking part in too much activity for a week.'

Willis moved away to make a note of the details, so Montgomery raised himself and sat back against the wall.

'I'll try,' he said. 'Provided I'm allowed to.'

Willis scribbled a few sentences, then looked up.

'I can only recommend. Name?'

'I'm Ryan O'Donnell,' Montgomery said.

Willis nodded. He removed a roll of bandages from a cupboard, then gestured to the guards in the doorway that they should sit down while he finished his work.

'In that case, Ryan,' he said, unwinding the bandages, 'welcome to Sumner Point jail.'

Frank Buchanan and Granville Coe quietly slipped into the cemetery outside Prospect Creek, as Ryan had suspected they would.

After leaving Sumner Point he had followed them at a distance until it had become clear they were returning to his home town. Although this was the one place he couldn't risk visiting, he hoped that Montgomery's sacrifice would buy him enough time to resolve his unfinished business.

The long journey gave him plenty of time to think through the implications of the information Montgomery had wrested off Granville, letting him come to the same conclusion as his quarries clearly had.

In an unconcerned manner they had gone straight to the small fenced-off area to the north of the town. Now they were walking up and down the rows of mounds. Granville had rested a shovel over one shoulder while Frank had drawn his six-shooter.

While they searched for one particular grave Ryan dismounted in a hollow. Then he made his way to the fence where he lay on his front and peered through the rails.

By the time he'd gained a position where he could see them, they were standing over three graves set back from the main group of mounds. After a brief debate Granville jabbed the shovel down into the furthermost grave. Then he gestured for Frank to go to the gate and keep watch. Frank did so without question.

The gate was fifty feet to Ryan's left. He waited in his hidden position until Frank was leaning back against a post and casually looking out for anyone coming from town before he started crawling towards him.

He was unsure of the reaction he would get, but this was the first chance he'd had to talk to Frank alone since leaving Sumner Point, and it was likely to be the last. He got to within a few feet of him when Frank stood up straight and peered round, clearly having heard his approach.

'Frank,' Ryan said levelly, 'don't react. We need to talk.'

For a moment Frank stood poised before his gaze darted down to see him. His eyes opened wide with surprise and for once he didn't sneer at him. Instead he looked to the other side of the cemetery where Granville was digging with strong, quick strokes.

Then he sidled along the fence to stand over Ryan. With a shrug he holstered his gun, then fixed his gaze on the town.

'You should have taken your punishment instead of coming looking for me. Now you're doubly doomed.'

'I had intended to, but then you told me that you're my brother . . . half-brother. So I have to stop you giving in to temptation.' Ryan considered Frank, noting that he still wasn't looking at him as he nervously faced the town. 'After all, you're the only kin I have left now.'

Frank firmed his jaw. 'Just say what's on your mind then go or I'll finish what I started in Sumner Point.'

'I have the copy of the letter Granville found in the railroad office. I've figured out what you and he figured out and what Sylvester Howie worked out earlier.'

Frank patted his pocket, nodding.

'Sylvester must have sent Edmond his watch to tell him he knew he'd provided details of the timing of the payroll's journey.'

Ryan looked at the grave where Granville had now moved the mound aside. His frantic digging had caused him to disappear down to his knees.

'And he died trying to uncover the truth about the conspiracy,' Ryan muttered, now finding that he couldn't stop the anger he'd kept at bay since he'd worked it out from bubbling over. 'And it involved three men nobody would suspect: Sheriff Jerry Harris, Deputy Foster Pilgrim, and railroad man

Edmond Shaffer.'

Frank joined him in snorting with contempt.

'They remained above suspicion because after they spirited the money away from the hapless Hudson Gilmore they blamed the even more hapless Casey O'Donnell.' Frank looked down at him and frowned. 'It must be hard on you knowing that you regained your reputation by saving Edmond's life when he was the one you should have killed.'

Ryan nodded. 'While the men I killed were the ones I should have supported. But then again you shot up those railroad men when they came looking for answers. And that means we have to stop the bloodshed by making sure the truth finally comes out.'

'The bloodshed I care about all happened in the past.'

'I know, and I can see it was hard for you having never known our father, but believe me: he wasn't worth knowing.'

'I won't get that chance now.' Frank looked at Granville and watched him as he continued digging. When he spoke his voice sounded honest. 'I only joined the marshal's mission to be there when he was found and so save him.'

Ryan too watched Granville dig. As Frank had come to Prospect Creek only six months ago, his first sighting of his father had probably been when he'd found his body. So he could appreciate how the situ-

Sumner Point jail by a legally sworn-in deputy, did you?'

'I did, and Deputy Pierce is fine. In fact he helped me to piece it together.'

'Then he'll be dealt with appropriately for failing in the duty he was paid to perform.'

Pilgrim leaned back in his chair and placed his hands together, fingertips touching as he awaited Ryan's explanation. Only the slight twitching of the index fingers betrayed the nervousness that he was trying to mask with his brusque manner.

'He's not the deputy you need to worry about.'

Pilgrim narrowed his eyes. 'What have you done with Frank Buchanan?'

'Nothing. He followed Montgomery and me to Sunflower City, as you ordered him to. But then he got side-tracked by another man into finding Edmond Shaffer and that turned into a hunt for the stolen payroll.'

'Who is this other man?'

'I don't know. But he's staying away from Prospect Creek, presumably deliberately, so he's probably known here.'

'Where did their hunt lead them?'

Ryan didn't reply immediately, enjoying making his revelation despite the urgent need to act. He stood and walked to the window where he craned his neck to look out of town, even though he couldn't see the cemetery from there.

'They're making away with it now after digging it up out of Sylvester—'

He didn't get to finish his explanation as Pilgrim leapt out of his chair, muttering an angry oath. Pilgrim stormed past Ryan to the door and Ryan had to run to catch up with him as he hurried outside to the hitching rail.

The sheriff didn't acknowledge him as he mounted up and set off at a gallop. Ryan followed at a more sedate pace, giving himself time to accept that the sheriff's reaction was the final proof that he had been the one who had ended up with the money.

When the cemetery came into view and he saw Pilgrim going straight to the graves in the corner he turned his thoughts to what he could do about it on his own.

Frank had spared him so that he could alert Pilgrim for no other reason than to set up a final confrontation and remove the last obstacle to their getting away with the money. He knew that Pilgrim wouldn't dare risk involving anyone else: it would be two men against one, with Ryan trapped in the impossible position of not wanting to side with anyone.

He was no nearer to solving his dilemma when he drew up at the cemetery gate to await Pilgrim's return from the open and now emptied grave of Sylvester Howie.

'Gone,' Pilgrim said as he kicked the gate open.

'Did they leave Sylvester's body?' Ryan asked, deciding to maintain the illusion that he hadn't figured out what Pilgrim's role in this situation was. When Pilgrim didn't reply he continued. 'Did you bury him there?'

'Who cares about Sylvester Howie?'

'We should. He could be the key to all this.'

Pilgrim stood by the gate and considered him. For a moment Ryan thought he might confide in him and perhaps even explain that he was wrong in his assumption, but then he shook himself and started to root around for tracks.

'The only important thing now is getting the money back.'

Ryan let him search until he found the spot where Granville and Frank had drawn up.

'Did you not even kill Sylvester?' he asked. 'Did he escape?'

Pilgrim followed the tracks, seeking to work out the way Granville and Frank had gone. When he ascertained that they'd ridden broadly west he relaxed and looked up at Ryan.

'I had my reasons for what I did and I'll explain them when this is over.' Pilgrim rubbed his jaw as he weighed up the situation. 'But I'm in a tricky position here and I need my former deputy to trust me enough to help me track down my other former deputy.'

'I note you're not offering to help me get out the

mess I'm in if I join you.'

'It's not my place to make such an offer and besides I know it wouldn't sway a man like you.'

Ryan smiled acknowledging the truth of his statement while also enjoying hearing that Pilgrim meant to act in the way he usually did.

'In that case I'll help you, and I can start by saving you time picking up the tracks. I know where they've gone.'

'I already know that.' Pilgrim sighed and tipped back his hat as he swung round to look west. 'It could only ever have been one place.'

A few more walls had fallen down in the buildings on the outskirts of Kendall Springs. That helped Ryan to see the two horses drawn up beside the derelict stables. An open wagon was also there, although Ryan couldn't see any sign of the stolen payroll on the back.

They stopped a hundred yards out of town to consider the scene.

'Do we try to sneak in?' Ryan asked.

'There's no point,' Pilgrim said. 'They'll be expecting us and we'll already have been seen.'

Ryan nodded. 'Then let's do this.'

Pilgrim returned the nod. Side by side they rode slowly into town.

As they approached the first building they gathered a better view of the inside of the stables. Its two standing walls wouldn't afford much cover for their quarries, if they were hiding there. But another dozen yards on they could see all of the interior.

Fifty feet from the wagon Pilgrim drew to a halt and glanced up and down the road. No other building had walls that were more than a few feet high, but this was high enough for two men to lie down and shoot them while remaining hidden. Pilgrim sidled closer.

'We keep moving on cautiously,' he said from the corner of his mouth, 'but when we make our move for cover, we do it quickly and we go to ground wherever we can.'

Ryan nodded, but while Pilgrim looked for the best place to seek refuge, he leaned forward in the saddle to look at the object that was now becoming visible beyond a wagon wheel.

'We can do that,' he said, 'or we could just go straight to the box they've left out on the road.'

Pilgrim followed Ryan's gaze, then urged his horse to move on at a walking pace.

'That's an obvious trap.'

'It is, but sometimes you have no choice but to spring them.'

Pilgrim grunted that he agreed, but he said nothing more until they reached the wagon, where he stopped to appraise the box. The closed box was around six feet long and three feet high and wide. It would have passed for a large coffin and, as it was soiled, it had probably been in the ground for a while.

'We'll do both,' Pilgrim said. 'I'll go to the side of the road while you see what's in the box. If they show their hand, get into the stables.'

Pilgrim no longer had the right to give him orders. But despite the fact that Ryan didn't trust him he found that he enjoyed their dealing with each other in the way they had during the short time they'd worked together. He nodded; then, while still moving slowly, he dismounted.

Pilgrim followed him and the two men stood together at the back of the wagon before, without a further word, Pilgrim moved off across the road at a steady patrolling pace. He headed for a burnt-down building that would afford him some protection, leaving Ryan to cover the ten paces to the box.

When he reached it Ryan took a deep breath; then, while looking out for movement from the corner of his eyes, he considered the box. It was essentially intact, although the lid had a large broken lock that had been shot apart.

Gaps between the planks let him see some of the interior. When he moved his head to the side he saw that something was lying within. He hadn't expected that the box would still contain the payroll, but there was only one way to find out the truth.

After checking that Pilgrim had reached the edge of the road, he hooked the toe of his boot underneath the rim.

He stood tall, ensuring he could see all parts of the road. Then he kicked upwards sending the lid flying, to reveal that within lay a smiling Granville Coe with a gun aimed up at him.

'Howdy, Ryan,' Granville said. 'You got here quickly.'

CHAPTER 15

'Where's Frank?' Ryan asked, staring down at Granville.

'He's here and he has a gun on Pilgrim,' Granville said, 'so the sheriff will throw his gun to the ground, as will you.'

As Granville moved up to a sitting position in the box, Ryan took a step backwards so that he could see Pilgrim while keeping Granville in view. Now knowing for sure that Frank was here, he couldn't help but look along the buildings, wondering where he'd gone to ground.

For several seconds the three men stood silently until, moving slowly, Pilgrim reached for his gun then tipped it out of its holster. Ryan followed his action but, like Pilgrim, he allowed the gun to drop at his feet where he could get to it easily.

Granville didn't appear concerned by their obvious caution; he clambered out of the box, then stood upright.

'So now we can end this,' Ryan said, 'as you wanted us to do.'

Granville nodded, then moved around Ryan to stand beside the wagon. He considered him, then Pilgrim across the road.

Ryan turned to him. As that position put his back to the main bulk of the town where Frank was probably hiding, Pilgrim didn't move. Granville smiled, suggesting he'd accepted he couldn't distract both men.

'I will,' he said. 'But you, alone and unarmed, can do nothing.'

'Sheriff Pilgrim and I will stop you. Then we'll return the money to the railroad.'

Granville raised an eyebrow. 'You know the sheriff's here to reclaim the money for himself, don't you?'

'I won't listen to your lies.'

Ryan glared at Granville, trying to appear confident in keeping Pilgrim on his side for now. In response Granville shook his head, then looked at Pilgrim across the road.

'Will you admit to the truth?' he called.

Pilgrim said nothing; and instead he settled his stance.

'So,' Ryan said when it became clear that Pilgrim wouldn't give Granville the satisfaction of replying, 'you and Frank are sharing the money, are you?'

147

'The sons of Casey O'Donnell should get the money, but that doesn't—' Granville broke off, his gun swinging round to aim across the road.

Ryan followed his gaze to see that Pilgrim had made his move while Granville had been deep in conversation. Pilgrim bent to scoop up his gun, then hurled himself at the short wall of the building beside him.

Granville loosed off a shot at his tumbling form, but the slug sliced into the top of the wall as Pilgrim dropped from view. Granville uttered an angry oath, then jerked the gun back to aim it at Ryan. He shook his head warning Ryan not to take him on, then beckoned for him to back away from his gun on the ground.

His gaze was so resolute that Ryan did as ordered and took steady steps backwards until his legs slapped against the box. As he stood beside the box Granville backed away to the corner of the wagon nearest the stables.

There he rested his gun against the edge of the wagon and aimed at the spot where Pilgrim had gone to ground. With Granville's attention no longer on him, Ryan considered his position.

His gun was three long paces away and he doubted he could reach it before Granville turned his gun on him, but then again Granville could have shot him by now if he'd wanted to.

Then Granville's last words came back to him.

148

He shook himself to dismiss the wild thoughts they gave him, but when he replayed what Granville had said through his mind he was sure he hadn't misheard.

It also explained everything.

As if Granville had sensed that Ryan had made the connection that had eluded everyone so far he looked at him, smiled, then looked beyond him down the road. His gaze tracked to the right suggesting he was watching someone, presumably Frank, move position and a few moments later a gunshot blasted as Pilgrim fired at Frank, although the sheriff kept himself out of sight.

Ryan reckoned this was the best moment to test his theory and he ran for his gun. Granville watched him, but he didn't turn his gun away from Pilgrim. So, on the run, Ryan gathered up the weapon then ran on into hiding beside the wagon at the opposite end to Granville.

He swung round in time to see Frank hurrying towards the cover of a collapsed wall fifty yards down the road. He had several yards left to run to reach it when Pilgrim darted up.

A gunshot blasted and Frank stumbled, although Ryan was unsure whether he'd been hit as he then fell from view behind a low-lying pile of burnt wood. Pilgrim followed his progress and he fired a second time.

As his shot kicked ash from the wood he started to

drop down, but he had stayed up for several seconds, giving Granville enough time to take careful aim. He fired. A grunt sounded and Pilgrim dropped from view with a hand rising to clutch his bloodied shoulder.

A moment later a heavy thud sounded. With a satisfied murmur Granville ran out from the wagon and hurried across the road.

'Stop!' Ryan warned, but his demand didn't slow Granville, who merely glanced at him as he passed.

'You know you won't fire,' he called over his shoulder as, from further down the road Frank looked up to appraise the situation.

Frank got to his feet and vaulted lithely over the woodpile, showing he hadn't been injured. He joined Granville in running to the building where Pilgrim had gone into hiding. Frank was twenty feet behind Granville when Granville reached a position where he should be able to see the wounded sheriff.

'You'll stop this!' Ryan shouted after them, although to his horror he found that he couldn't make his arms move to raise his gun, neither did Granville heed his warning.

Granville looked over the short wall into the building. He settled his stance, picked his target with calm confidence, and then fired twice in rapid succession.

A few moments later Frank reached his side and together the two men looked down at the presumably dead form of Sheriff Pilgrim. Then they both swung round to face Ryan.

'Obliged you didn't stand in our way, Ryan,' Frank said, tipping his hat. 'But I hope you're not expecting to get a share of the payroll.'

'I'm not,' Ryan said. 'But then again you won't be getting it either. The money's going back to the railroad.'

Frank narrowed his eyes. 'You don't mean that. You didn't try to save Pilgrim.'

'I know he wanted it for himself and so he had to be stopped, but we know it's a different matter between the three of us.' Ryan spread his hands. 'We can work this out.'

Frank shook his head. 'We can't. I killed Alexander.'

'You did, but I reckon you never meant to go that far. You were angry and even though you've been trying not to show it, that act quenched your need to hit back. So the sons of Casey O'Donnell don't need to fight amongst themselves no longer.'

'Family don't mean nothing. We shared a father, nothing else.'

Ryan smiled. Feeling more in control now that Frank was responding to his attempts to talk him round, even if he wasn't accepting his viewpoint, he took a steady pace forward.

'You're right. Family isn't everything, but perhaps the fact we've both been lawmen could mean something. We deputies should stick together.'

Frank waved a dismissive hand at him, then looked at Granville for his reaction. Granville was smiling, suggesting he'd understood the full meaning of Ryan's offer.

With Granville saying nothing Frank raised his gun to aim at Ryan's chest. Despite the threat Ryan found that he couldn't raise his own weapon.

'Don't make me fire,' Frank said. 'We can leave you here and you can go back to jail. That can be the end to this.'

'It can't. The sons of Casey O'Donnell should do the right thing and if one of them won't, it's up to the others to keep him in line.'

Granville snorted, making Frank glance at him before he firmed his gun hand.

'You're in no position to make threats, Ryan.'

Ryan glanced at his own gun, then with slow movements he opened his hand and let it fall to the ground.

'I wasn't talking about me,' he said. He paced over the gun and slowly walked towards Frank. 'I was talking about you. Do the right thing for once. Face up to the son who won't.'

'What you. . . ?' Frank winced, then swung round to face Granville, although he kept his gun on Ryan. He gulped before he spoke again. 'I know you're not Marshal Granville Coe, but who are you?'

In response Frank received a wink as well as a gun that rose steadily to aim at him.

'He's Sylvester Howie,' Ryan called as he continued to advance. 'Pilgrim didn't kill him. He got away. So you now have a decision to make. You can follow your outlaw half-brother or you can follow your lawman half-brother. I know which direction you'll enjoy the most.'

Frank stood in open-mouthed shock; he didn't react even when Sylvester levelled his aim at his chest. Ryan couldn't blame him. He was still just as shocked as Frank was at losing a brother only then to gain one, and now two.

But one of those gains had clearly followed the direction everyone expected the sons of Casey O'Donnell to take, and so he was left to hope that the other would make the choice he and Alexander had.

'Is this true?' Frank murmured.

'Sure,' Sylvester said with a glance at his gun. 'The only question is: what are you going to do about it?'

Frank lowered his head. He stared at the ground, murmuring to himself and taking deep breaths, but then with a great roar of anger he hurled himself at Sylvester. His sudden movement caught Sylvester by surprise and before he could shoot Frank grabbed his arm and bundled him backwards for a pace.

Ryan jerked forward, aiming to help Frank, but then he thought better of joining in the skirmish. He turned on his heel and hurried back to his discarded gun. Sounds of the struggle came from behind him, but he put them from his mind and concentrated on reaching the gun.

The moment he slapped a hand on the weapon he turned quickly and swung the gun up. He was confronted by the sight of Frank lying on the ground, pole-axed, and Sylvester's back as he walked away.

Sylvester paced across the road, then stepped over the short wall into the building beside the one in which Pilgrim had fallen. He holstered his gun, then bent to pick up two bulging saddlebags. He placed them on the wall and gathered up two more. Only then did he look up and smile.

'Bring those bags over here,' Ryan ordered.

'We all have the same problem,' Sylvester said, his tone unconcerned. 'We're all brothers. I can't shoot you and you won't shoot me. That means you get to walk away from this, but it also means you can't stop me from leaving with the money. You can join me though, if you like.'

Ryan firmed his gun hand, finding that Sylvester was right. With every passing moment his determination to stop his kin leaked away. On the ground Frank shook himself and pushed himself up to a sitting position.

'We're not coming,' he murmured.

'That's your choice,' Sylvester said.

Sylvester clambered over the wall to stand in the road. Then he shuffled the bags on to his shoulders one at a time before he set off across the road. He didn't balk at putting his back to Frank and when he

154

reached the wagon he smiled at Ryan.

'No, it's your choice,' Frank called. 'If you put those bags on the wagon, I'll kill you.'

'You won't shoot you own kin again and neither will I.'

Frank snorted a laugh of bravado, but Ryan saw the uncertainty in his eyes that said Sylvester was right about him too. Then Sylvester's comment registered. He'd made the same point twice, as if to reassure himself.

'Except that's not true,' Ryan said. 'You hated our father because you thought it was his fault you'd become a wanted man, so you saved your skin by telling Hudson Gilmore where he could find him.'

'That was different,' Sylvester muttered.

'It wasn't because now we all know that our father had nothing to do with the raid, after all. You got him killed for nothing.'

Sylvester stomped to a halt. He shrugged the bags on his shoulder, looking as if he was working out how to swing them up on to the wagon, but then with a sudden gesture he lowered his shoulders and let them fall.

Before the bags hit the ground he turned at the hip, his gun coming to hand, but he didn't get to complete the move before Frank fired. His gunshot sliced into Sylvester's side.

Sylvester staggered sideways for a pace, then tripped over a discarded bag which sent him reeling into the wagon. He grabbed hold of the backboard and righted himself.

'You take after our father,' he murmured, his breath coming in pained gasps.

He moved to turn his gun on Frank again, but this time two simultaneous gunshots slammed into his chest from Ryan's and Frank's guns.

The slugs made Sylvester stand up straight. He stood swaying for a moment. He fixed both men in turn with his gaze, his knitted brow showing his surprise, as if he couldn't believe that the sons of Casey O'Donnell would actually be on the side of the law.

Then he keeled over, to lie sprawled across the bags. He twitched once, then lay still.

For a long minute the two surviving men stood in silence, watching the breeze rustle the flaps of the dropped bags that so many men had died over. Ryan was the first to speak.

'We're not going to fight over this now,' he said, 'are we?'

'Nope,' Frank said. 'Killing two brothers was one too many for me.'

With that acceptance of having done wrong in the past, even if he'd done the right thing in the end, Ryan moved over to sit beside Granville. Presently Frank joined him. The two men sat with their dead brother as the sun lowered and the wind got up and spiralled flurries of ash and dust down the road.

'I never knew this brother,' Ryan said after a while.

156

'And in his case I'm glad.'

'And in my case?'

Ryan looked up. 'That's yet to be decided.'

Frank nodded. 'I'll settle for that.'

CHAPTER 16

'It's good to be free so soon,' Montgomery Pierce said. He took a long pace out through the prison gates, then stretched tentatively, showing that his injury was still healing.

'I'm obliged for what you did,' Ryan said. He nodded to the two guards at the door, who were staying back for now, in deference to his voluntary action of turning himself in. 'You took a big risk.'

'It was worth it to get answers.' Montgomery raised his eyebrows, questioning whether Ryan had in fact obtained them.

Ryan gestured to the open wagon standing on the main road where Frank broke off from keeping a careful eye on the box in the back to give a brief nod.

'We did, and after Frank's taken the stolen payroll back to the railroad he'll tell you who Marshal Granville Coe really was. Hopefully that'll explain my actions too.'

'And perhaps help to reduce your sentence?'

'I don't know. That's for others to decide. But bearing in mind the wrong so many others did in stealing the payroll in the first place, my small dereliction of duty to help a man who turned out to be innocent sounds less significant all the time.'

Montgomery nodded. 'When I find someone who'll listen I'll speak up for you. And it looks as if Frank might join me.'

Ryan was still unsure about the latter, but he mustered a snort of laughter.

'I'll be grateful for anything you can do. After all, we deputies have to help each other out.'

Montgomery patted him on the back, then stepped back to let the guards take control of him. As Montgomery headed over to the wagon, Ryan looked around, enjoying what would be his last moments of freedom for a while.

Even so, he hoped that he wouldn't have to wait for the full two years before he could return to Prospect Creek. As a guard clamped a firm hand on his shoulder, he caught Frank's eye as he sat in the wagon.

'I'll see you soon,' Frank called without any hint of the malice that had always been in his voice whenever he'd spoken to him previously.

'And I'll see you too,' Ryan said, finding that, to his surprise, he would welcome trying to get to know the only remaining member of his family.

159

They looked at each other and Frank's pensive expression showed that he was rooting around for the right thing to say. Ryan also felt he should say something more, but like his half-brother he wasn't sure what it was.

When the guard drew him away, Ryan walked backwards to the door, giving himself time to think.

'And then maybe,' Frank shouted when he reached the gate, 'the sons of Casey O'Donnell can work together to keep the peace.'

'Brothers should help each other out,' Ryan said with a smile before the gate closed.